An Dantomine Eerly

AN DANTOMINE EERLY

J.R.D. MIDDLETON

DARK COAST PRESS
www.darkcoastpress.com
| Seattle |

Published by Dark Coast Press
FIRST PRINTING

Dark Coast Press Co.
6201 15th Avenue NW #330
Seattle, WA 98107, U.S.A.
www.darkcoastpress.com

First U.S. paperback edition published 2010
This book is also available in electronic format

isbn-13: 978-0-9844288-0-9
isbn-10: 0-9844288-0-1
Library of Congress Control Number (lccn): 2010921407

Cover painting by Pierre-Cécile Puvis de Chavannes,
Le Rêve; 1883

Cover design by Blake Marquis
Text design by Matthew J. Novak
Illustrated text by Rachel Dorothy Blowen

Printed at Thomson-Shore, Inc.

Manufactured in the United States of America

10 9 8 7 6 5 4 3 2 1

Acknowledgements

This book would not have been possible without the hard work of its editors Aaron S. Talwar and Andrew Legendre. A very special thanks to Rick Middleton and Jaidev Talwar for their miraculous support. Thank you to Jacquelyn Benson, Patrick Brownson, and Jared Bowers for additional reading; Matthew Novak for text design; and Blake Marquis for the original cover design. A debt of gratitude to Tom Moulton for my time spent at the Four Winds cottage at Monhegan Island, ME, where the first drafts of An Dantomine Eerly were written. And to my family, thank you.

For Rachel

CONTENTS

Who, if not the single wind, is sighing
Alone here with distant diamonds dying?
Whose sob so near myself is taking place?

PAUL VALERY; Fragments from
The Youngest of the Fates.

I AM HERE NOW ALONE in my hole, my portal, my awfully shiny prison, . . . a bay window facing the Atlantic shore. In our time together I will show you what singular minds do when tossed fuse lit into violent twilight, indiscriminate fire, and that inevitable result that arises—a slow, bobby, buoyant wade through blackness. I come to you in salvage of a gallant fall, dropped from the idea of Heaven through a sky of abject constellations, upon the thin wire where weary definitions of earth and life hang. I orient, obtain for balance, admittedly unsuccessful; but that, I think, is hardly the point, because once that balance is questioned it become weightless, no matter the gravity of which it weighs.

I welcome you. Amusements are coming alongside raps-upon-the-back, slaps of joy, and as much as I may assure, long scripts of true endearment. Believe me, we have the same scars. You and I are bound by familiar bonds of sickness. Sit if you'd like, it'll warm my cozy little worm's nest. My heart will pump precious vital beats onto your efforts upon our meeting, even if they are some of my last. I'll give them to you, that is the importance of what I have to tell you: the story of my life abruptly torn from me, then ended. I'll provide fuel and light the best I can, to the best of me yet. My smiles are all frowns, for when I am upside down you turn me upright, mouth agape, and you must push through the horror. I did, and that is how I came to know An Dantomine Eerly, whom some would call the Boatman or Bringer of Death, whom others might call an Ascended Master, and whom others further still could view as an obscurity of Intention somewhere between Angel, Principal, or Seraph, respectively. So, focus your view, whether it be on this twilight, fire, laughter, or fright, as I wind these satin strings of language, desperately mad, and at times seldom celebratory of the exchange we are now to endure.

ONE

From the earliest time I wanted to push my whole face deep into my eyes and sleep eternally in the womb of my mind, images of our world fading from sight and memory. Instead, there were these endless symphonies composed only of sirens that surrounded me from all around. Though this pained me, I slowly learned to spend myself with the currency of their silences. It was poetry, really, that brought me from the ruthless perturbations of that which emerges and that which fades to the orchestral mystery of the inner globules and the outer worlds, revealing, within all that screaming, the order beneath it.

Down on the earth, on some world Avenue, I was late for an obligation. If I had checked I would've learned that I was in fact early. Early for a feast. That sounds quite decadent, don't you think?

The aesthetic crimes of neon-signs and halogen beamed their bath-confessionals from the vacant sides of liquor store lots, gas stations, and, farther up in the distance, the sky-world of highway crossbridges, off-ramp dining holes, and worn out truckstops. The hazy illuminations sank dusk into the ground the way pins and roofing nails tack bedsheets to crackhouse windows. And when I happened to slide down into those tubs of yellow-gray light the continuing symptoms of the womb-of-mind sleep that by birth had already been denied me began to surge, to circle and ensnare, to pull at my unknowing that lay somewhere beneath my skin, urging me to squeeze my whole self into tiny holes poked through the most worn out parts of my anus and knees, hoping I'd spray out onto the pavement or at least dribble off into the street. "Either way," I thought, "relinquish yourself to eternity, or flee into the falseness that lay ahead."

My face turned from the side streets, and with the last of the light smoldering down across the detritus of that scene, I prepared and became the change to evening. A settling darkness that begot the concrete avenues, billboard faces, distorted smiles blown out by the murder-light, the whole rotting idea of town; the gray dream. Where night had settled lightly I arrived, and stood before a deco façade, apparently, for a meal, and if I could've torn through the fabric of that street right then, walk through it—not on it, as we do the air—to disappear and spill out on another paper-thin side of perception, believe me I would have, but many things still blocked me from such a passage.

The oak doors opened with relative ease, though they were heavy. Inside, climbing the dark stairwell in the one-sided tinge of old copper lanterns, I reached the second floor. Dust demurred between blue wall and open corridor, and through it, down the other end, more glowing copper pieces and other ornaments arose, casting a whip of shadow off lapping light out across the deep recesses of the hall. When I walked into the foyer, approaching the door, a house maid arrived meagerly in the door frame. Her head was faced down, and she pulled a silver circle from the white fold of her apron, checking her timepiece. She glanced back a furtive and disapproving look. "Can I not come in?" I asked her quietly, moving with courtesy toward the door, when she stepped in front of me, skirt hem swaying at the fronts of her knees, saying to me: "No, goddon'tyouhaveanysensewiththesekindsof things?" Hesitant. "May I sit and wait then?" She nodded toward a bench against the wall, then vanished.

Sitting there, other guests arrived. I heard them come through the downstairs foyer, then almost instantly up the stairs. Each of them passed by me and brought with them Ghosts, like cloaks, through the large apartment door; and when their coats were taken they were greeted and shown inside. Hurriedly! While I sat there, fastened to a weight! They all wore these cloaks. Some were heavy and coarse, some light, over-worn linen, some shined from within like lamp lights, some were dimmed with the assurance of beliefs, and some trembled from the ~~coward~~ cowered body that curled underneath. Only after they had all come through was I called for, not by name, but by the glare of the churlish maid who saw me seated still on the bench through the empty passageway. She held open the door, perfumed with an odious sentiment (I smelled it as I passed, a piss, a brine), and proceeding again through another narrow corridor I entered through the main room where I headed straight for my seat at the end.

The cloaked guests sat facing their plates, ready to feast at the long table in the center of the room, draped in red. Walking along the length of it, I caught their faint hands nervously slipping underneath the blood colored cloth, saw their thin lips lather, they hunched over the table as packs of black-leather junkies would crouch over the thick thighs of a porcine whore laid out before them, newly dead, still wet with sweat but her plumbing dry, ready for the spit of the angels to ease along her last impossible offering. Passing that, I sat, unsure of the guests, why I was there, and what type of order I was in danger of disrupting.

Upon the table, bowls, plates, and glasses spread around an enormous platter of silver, filled to its brim with pounds of meat. There were shrimp, salads, pastas, peppers, vin du Rhône, Bordeaux, pinot, grapes, berries, nuts, beans, corn, mushrooms stuffed with peppered crab, assorted breads. As well laid the appropriate cutleries: knives, forks, spoons, the assorted picks, hooks, scalpels, cleavers, clamps, and the odd personal effects of our guests whom are preferred for their cunning in dismemberment, sure, but are also, I am told, rife with sporty talk and tasteful presence! There were laughs! Unsettling laughs, rapacious, reputable. I took from the platter and reached into warm bowls, filling my plate quickly. I started to eat and became dizzy, forgetting everything that had happened before it.

Gulped down glasses of wine in between sampling and shoveling the food, then a break, to pour again the swirling red from the bottle, burying my face deep in the glass. The wine began to take effect; it reached into the various corners of my body. The wreck of dialogue converged along pre-disposed lines of contact and rose in a cloud from the center of the table, up, and outwards, causing the dust to dance in the chandelier and lamp light. "Who are these people?" was a question that churned continuously in the back of my mind. There was dust, the smell of tobacco and liquor, hurt lovers, wild-eye. . . . Their mouths moved, but oceans crashed and landscapes erupted slowly; I didn't even know what language they were speaking. No matter. I heard tanks plowing through tree lines, satyrian gut-speak, I wasn't about to let it make me meek. Scanned their features, each face in a cage of negative space, forming and emerged, only slightly. . . . So, I downed more wine, and the abstract clamor continued. The dark carnival commenced.

Night draped depthless sheets in the tall windows lining the open room. The metabolism of the conversation was quickening, diverging, and re-convening, and that same laughter grew louder, in tide-rhythm. Some had stopped, but I kept on eating, pulling new gifts from the cornucopia. In fact, in all truth, my chewing and sipping had kept me from hearing too clearly what came from whom and how they got to where they were, both in their own lives and the life of their banter. Opportune to speak I poised, then passed, and then poised again, when something caught my attention, . . . the kerned, purple perianths of many loose violets dotted the rim of the silver platter. I backed my chair out and my glass sloshed as I stood at the helm of the table, peering across. *"Are those fucking violets?"* I yelled. The sounds from every mouth that clouded the table and engulfed the room ceased. Immediately, a wine cramp stung my brain and the entire back of my head burned as the torrent of me breathing again tore through the silence.

". . . well, they must've eaten quickly," I thought. All of the plates were there, shining and untouched. Silverware gleamed in respective placements, aligned on rows of white napkins, next to clear glasses. The central platter was clean and void of meat. Nothing moved, no guts sucked in, poked out, no bodies were growing full, and, to be sure, no violets. From the long wood table, the empty bowls and bare trays, fresh laid plates, and the big platter, I sat compromised in silence. The corral had gone, seemingly, at the moment of my mere utterance. It was strange, perceiving myself from without. The more I viewed that bare table and the pristine accoutrements the more they stretched out and pushed themselves in, becoming portraits of themselves. The more I approached the surrounding details they emerged from obscure to precise and the movement of this approach, the gazing flight down long planes and around round corners, accelerated and could not hold that precision which was occurring, itself further obscured by the arbitrariness of all its definition. It was this, myself stretched so thin, that fled away, until all movement snapped back into my very own stillness. There I was, blood through the body, electric fingers scintillated by the flow of an unseen river, still and in flight, frantic and calm, within annihilation, yet whole, budding with negation, unbecoming my own assumption. At a table, a chair, and in that chair, a figure, and in that figure?

There was no man bouncing off of storefront windows in moonlit fragments and reflections. If you saw him, well then you imagined him. You imagined him exactly how he passed you. You made up gusting wind, that perfect speed, the weight with which he strolled down the concrete. You made the smell, familiar, or foul, you made the worn face, the shadow of the shoulders, and the broad back made beastly by the moon. So in a sense he was there for you, in relation to—, or more correctly, only there like that, to you, because of you.

Oh. Oh, oh. "Step upon the bricks like a piano, cry on them like a violin." "What the fuck are you talking about?" "Hey, look up there at the colorless shades." Some waxy garbage, transistors and soiled clothes. "A really swell arrangement sits behind that building right ahead." "What does that mean, exactly?" "Well what do you think it is?" "A great labyrinth of animal-human architecture." "I think it's a whorehouse, it's a whorehouse isn't it." "It's a long road out of this fucking place, that's what it is." "Oh, it's funny, that humans only need a few basic things to surv—," "Human?" "Yeah yeah, human. You know, . . . water, blood, shit, that shoddy neuro-quilt of outmoded ideas?" "Ah yes, human!"

"Oh. Oh, oh, but you left something out." "What a night out!" "What? No, I said you left something out. What if I told you that I believe something other, something else entirely. . . ." "Do you believe, or suspect? Assume, hope, or transfigure? Intonate, postulate, or correlate?" "Stop, please. . . ." "Do you will or do you pray or do you just masticate all day is what I'm asking?" "Again, you're not answering." "No one wants to hear what you believe anyway." "You're missing the whole god damned point." He turned and snapped back at me with his eye winked and his hand cocked into the shape of a gun, "exactly."

"How do I take the appallingly perfect consistency of the instantaneous production of moments? (Question:

How do I suffer perfection? Answer: Perfectly. Or until it is perfect)."

"You know, I'd love to know all the little intricate tricks of being. You know I'd love to find them." "But you can't. You can't handle the intricacies of life that they call magic." "Don't say that." "What, that you ruin everything's potential?" "I thought I was everything's potential!" "Then reason is, or ruin is, is—, I'm tired."

"Oh, so what, you want to charm laughter out of a twine basket and make it dance upon the world? You want to sway that diamond on its head, don't you, you blathering prick? '*Ew*,' it says to itself, '*could I make life lead itself into a hypnosis of pleasure and daft music?*' Ha! You'd love to boom with laughter and see the living, see the dead, see the living, there are no others, it is desert, it is an imploded landscape, it is a worn out nightmare that is extremely exclusive. So sing! Make the chubby music! Sing sing sing sing sing baby, sing it out. Sing out that good ol' oily shit! Help me! *. . .ountry tis of thee, sweet land of ha-da-da, ha-ha!*" "There's violence on the horizon! *. . .umpin' in puddles of blue blood BAH-DA BAH-DA BAH-DA DA-DAH. . .*" "The horizon! Ha! Follow it arduously enough and you'll ram yourself in the ass, man!"

"Hate them ♫ Hate them ♫ Hate them when they call your name. When they grip your hand and thank you for surviving."

"Love them ♫ Love them ♫ Love them when they come for you, because they are coming in a Grave Way."

"*Love?* Ten thousand boots are readying for your face your ideas your heart your wife your children your house your whiskey your cum your sun your salt wind and secluded shore and there are ten thousand more with poor reading levels pushing back tears and some even pushing confusing erections against the desks of Sergeants convinced of the Enemy and ready to sign. Pens tremble in lost hands! *(A' boom boom.)* And now they're a coming! *(A' boom boom.)* But! *(Clear that jackboot rustle and hear the birds telling you that)* when it is all taken from you, when the grown infants come with guns fumbling tidbits of the ideas of our elders, when you wake one morning to find that not-too-far eyes dot the horizon and that medals and tags and rank pins shine unbelievably in the sun, believe it, red mouths wet to rip you apart. You'll have to rise despite the collapse and go meet the hollow ones who refract the sun so unawares. Rejoice for now! In this, your possession of it all!"

I rose to meet the night. The city's mouth hid me away behind its row of rotting gums. It hid all others away as well, not another in sight. Even the cats were asleep in their window frames. It had rained, the street smoked from its sewers, and a mild wind carried through me, onto the next rogue straggler, . . . though I don't know that there was one. Others would be rising for work soon, but I never saw one. I knew cars sat on every freeway in the country, that priests sat on toilets shaped like the mouths of pouting children, politicians on people, and the dildo of their invented language, that tankers bobbed in the Atlantic waters, and that fear draped down over all working hearts, . . . but really I knew nothing. The street, I saw the street, knew the street. Even through the screeching of the strings I knew that street. In between the repetitious clicks of my walking thought livened the air, and in it, heel, and brick, I bounced, danced, and floated up, then back down again.

As far as the eye could see—emptied intersections, automatic traffic lights, corporate signs ruining midnight, gray fumed dancers above colonial sewer grates, cries absent of their widow, worry absent of its clown, warmth absent of its mother, streets shooting outwards, begging politely for absent revolts, for rough, spontaneous usage and wondrous heavy petting; warehouse skeletons were decaying and new groups of weeds were budding up, a new sense of absence was growing in all things experiencing different levels of usage and in all things that cope with being forgotten—

I am the blue infant of the warm & early
Morning you Rise to each day,
I am the blue infant exposed tonight. ...I
am, too, bound here with you, in your
Mournful Void.

Still. Singing arose. ". . . Who was that? Who's there?" I shouted into the empty street. Slowed my step, turned, and looked around. I would've said for him to show himself but I was certain there was no one, never for a moment had I sensed another body.

"I am the blue infant exposed to night. I am, too, bound here with you, in your mournful void. A blue infant? A blue infant, a blue infant. Of a warm & early morning? A blue infant and a warm and early morning . . . What Mournful Void?"

Lounge singers wailed in places I could not be. Wolves slept away in deep forests that sat at the foot of intraversable mountains. Welfare clerks doled out checks in offices that could not stand one kiss. Men were children in their heads, retracing the many steps that led them back to the womb; or at least their wives' red heavens. Bombs dropped in Iraqi markets and Basra's kindest bedrooms. The Mothers sang and prayed. The Disappeared did not return. The sirens did not cease. Gay prostitutes bent over dirtied ovens and squatted over worn linoleum in places I was not, nor would ever be. My worry was their worry. Life had a pulse and its pulse had ceased, at least for me. I can't say when, but it faded from me a long time ago. "But now this," I thought, "now there's this, . . . a truly novel occurrence, a mind! Of mine, of mine!" Phenomenal, petrified.

I staggered in the street hoping to see someone. No not *hoping* to see someone, I knew there was no one. I knew where this man, this being, this bearer of voice wasn't and that was anywhere in front of me, in the sense that you and I understand such things. Looking upon the cold night more and more, there was nothing. Breathing lightly, so as to stop even the littlest wisp of fog from leaving my mouth, there was nothing. Oh of *course* there wasn't anything! How delightful it was. How pitifully, ruthlessly, maniacally god-damned, god-feared, god-absently delightful it was. A mind, "of mine, of mine! Speaking poetics silently, only to myself." Draping the crazed interior cushion of a skull; only to me only to me came the strange poetry—

How many know of that first night out
in the cold when he told her never to worry?
How many closed snow roads produced quietly
perfect miracles on the nights the fearful
closed their eyes and trembled beneath old
blankets hoping to find a belief that might
relieve their fright?

Calling out one more time, I knew there'd be no response, and as I moved on from the street the possibilities began to pop and twirl in my blood. Yellow archs suggested times past, not yet had, or those that roll over, and over, again and again. I stepped cautiously along the wet bricks but stopped looking, letting those enunciations ring through me freely, an honest to God smile stretched across my face. In this pause, this innerving, kinetic flow of ghost air, I smiled. *Freely! Do you understand what that means?* This carried me as I strung my steps together through the streets!

The night brings more disturbing news. Received a letter today, regarding a colleague of mine from long ago. These memories come to me from an earlier era, one that appears tonight as a sweet, young dream. That time seems such a world away now, here whiskey cooled, as the house protects me from the batter of wind.

My old colleague Gardon, is dead. So it seems the anarchist finally got his fight, the lawless in him met the Law, and the restless Traveler travels forth past new posts and garrets, in through the low worlds and up the new heights.

As I was told, Gardon was drunk one evening at a gathering when he rose and began to read aloud. Some field town outside of Boise. They say he was a little wild, a bit provocative that particular night, and just started getting down to it, with all the yelling, melodious howling, long whispers with those standing close enough to get caught up in his danger, slinging his love slander, ordering hits on the Presidents of Everything, and just before he saw it coming that barn was aglow with torches. The air became heavy under a circle of fire, heck-yells filling the spaces between men; 'burn 'em!' they yelled, and 'through dar dust, tar murn!' They were cruel, and swift. The fuse had been lit.

They carried him out to a cornfield and hoisted him up on a barn plank, tarring and feathering him until he was completely covered and maimed, they jeered from behind their wall of cotton-swathed flame, as a crowd gathered of people from the town. They then spent the night drumming up all sorts of wonderful emanations on the various slips of his seditious tongue, his heresies to roofbeams and the Holy streams that flow through their wax fields of Livelihood. In the end, when all was said and done, the commoners thanked the murderous patrons for the performance of a public service.

My poor friend, in the age where we find ourselves hung upon such cruel fates one wonders why risk saying anything at all. And as you rest, and I fear to know what state that may be (it's over now), I refrain from one more word upon one more page, save this tame personal journal and its reflection on universal events that make a stormy eve and the endless grace of my wife seem all a man should need. I'll write no more, construct no more, invent, no more. I am through with all the shit. I can only care about survival now, we've been receiving threats lately ... and now this violence ...

For where'er he lay I can at least laugh tonight, with the suspicion that he is giving it right and giving it straight to that guardian of The Gate, The River, Mount, Temple, Tomb, The Mind. Rest this night, good friend, and let my sorrow bring you rest, as your death lends us life, our most unfortunate exchange.

I hadn't any control of my thermostat. I became so fearful of it that I could hear from any area of the apartment exactly when it clicked on. Once it began I never knew when it would stop, and as soon as the musty smell of the heater core spread itself throughout the apartment it brought sleeplessness with it, attacking with the rising sting of fevers and prejudice against my clothing.

"The heat eats me." In the psychosis of near-sleep I'd batter myself by repeating various phrases, usually it started with "the heat eats me." I'd lay awake exhausting every combination of the term: "The meat hates me," "The man baits me," "Gleam fatesie," "Gloom, Fate, see?" "Giants are raising me," "Gangalagangala gate-speak," "harem fuck timespeed—me please."

". . . Take me away." I was drifting. "*Away*," and there, someone drifted with me.

As she approached the bed I grew nervous and sick. I hadn't seen this for some time. Before her eyes, I saw pouty, light red lips come towards me from the foot of the bed. Somehow, I knew them; lips kissed so often . . . time escaped me. They pursed intently, soon caring after the teary wounds of my eyes, driving back past sweat and into the salt of my own tears. My hands reached, slid, and obtained; she pressed her lips in, dragging softly down the neck.

"You're gentle to me," she whispered, ethereal palms searched their way across my hips. Where do they rest in the moments where I am so taken? I emerged from beneath the blanket of her body which had been tossed on me from above. She crawled upon me and disrobed.

When the moonlight hit in gleaming silver, her back arched, blazoned; a slender line descending down into the center of her wet fire. "That line," I said aloud. "Oh, that arched back is where I measure my despair!" It is the breaking back of us all that my hands slid down, along the liquid silver of night. From a distance, the far-off hill which I've departed rises, and with it my wish to return. But there she was, knelt above me, taking the fuck-drunk night's perfumed air in through her open nostrils, . . . flushing her breasts with the sentiment of her sex and pushing them out into space, . . . her areolas fluttering and opening up, . . . budding, bee-ravaged stamens swaying in the fields, . . . nipples thick and crying for love, . . . for real teeth marks and red hand prints, . . . for the abusive cursive of force, . . . her thighs stung all over with it, . . . my eyes knifed by her beating tits, her falling chest, . . . our coming spirit fucks, body thrusts.

"Now to the indulgence which only two from two times can make, in the wake of everything that was once alive, but is now dead."

And two bodies became one like a battered child running towards a closet.

I was awash with her. Make-up on the top, blood on the bottom. Tangled in her fibers, hanging on them, climbing into night. The nervous area of night. The pillowy corner. I rode there with her, through her.

Through the timeless ride there was a bright, peaking light, then, her deep exhale, bringing the earthly weight of her body down to rest on one delicious wet spot on my stomach.

She cried later as she spoke of suffering. Let out a bit about her fragile state, that what she hoped for changed with the different curses she broke under. And vivid dreams detailed bringing them their ends, like neat little packages, but she couldn't bear the responsibility of deciding what crimes deserved what deaths. We quit with the conversation, keeping sleep near for some time, flirting with its caress, slipping in and out, but never fully submerging ourselves in it. Our rub of bones and gritted teeth finally found their rest in the quiet that arose between each moan and baleful repeating breath.

When she rose, her shoulders were squared to the day slowly brightening in the window behind her; . . . dawn had begun. She knew what was to happen. Her teary eyes were vapid with fright. The light came in and she began to fade. It filled the room, spreading across her back robbed of its *vita lunaris*. The sun hit her scapulas, causing them to disappear—their leanness, their absolute fragility, gone—her delicate wings taken from her, taken from me. The day came up and spread unforgiving across her entire naked body. She looked up at me so longingly from inside those dying eyes, opening her mouth the faintest bit, her lips shriveled and dried, failing to sigh out her last goodbye. I reached for her, but in the resigned comfort of a habitual gesture, evidence we'd done this before.

So, away she went, way up, out the window, back through the sky, back to her insufferable days as whose-ever slave, back to her long and bright hell, that hell that she must fight through to be what she's able to be, at least for me, that Angel of Evening. And so she left me then, to roam in my tolerable days, scurrying through the dusk of dread into the intolerable night, which was easily made colder with each departure. So were my nights and so burned her days, separated until our next tryst against time and hate, and trading her hell for mine I waved goodbye as the last of her lovely wings melted on the rim of the nearing sun.

. . . from bright to dim, . . . bright to dim, I awoke, in a familiar light that spread through horizontal, half-closed blinds. I laid there still in disbelief. His or mine, whose mind was on that street with me? A ghostly hallucination caused by wine and levity? A Poem-self? Or was it Logos? Godhead? It had ceased since then, and just as before I knew that if I called to it or went around to seek it out that it would not answer. I tried to put it out of my head when a new mystery hit me. I rolled over and felt the space beside me in bed, empty, an emptiness I was used to, sure, but it never felt empty as in the case of someone's absence. Stirrings of the sacred-feminine, of shadow-play and silvery sex dreams, it was all there, faintly conjured, but it all ran through my hands the moment I tried to grasp any particular aspect of it.

Concerned, the previous worry faded and speechless contemplation grew in its place. The walls of the bedroom were covered with black, cursive writing. Lines sprawled of quotations, phrases, hints, tales, and poetry! Poetry, goddamnit! I scoured the lines and assumed at first that I had written it, even though I didn't remember writing a thing. Walked throughout the room, and ran my hand across the words in lateral slats of shade and sunlight spread along each wall. Within its intricacy was evidence of madness. Looked in wonder, inched closer, squinted my eyes, and it was that closer look that assured this was not my doing. Or that some of it was? It appeared as if a hundred voices had collided. It read like the first half of a dream and then devolved with the repetitive ranting of the daily mind. But it was not me, I would never think in such a language, such terms, and I would certainly not scrawl my own tongue all over my own walls, "no, these words are not mine, of course they aren't. I didn't do this, they were of this thing which is now with me. But, how? Was someone in here?" suspecting for a moment that I had been followed home from the street. My focus returned to the walls. Some of the words were familiar, but so much of it I couldn't recognize or understand in origin or meaning. Much of it, truly, was inconceivable.

"Up the brick atop the palas leaves—from there the lamplight shined! on me shine on me, . . . take me to the Gulf, come take me to the, sweet tits what'd you—come to thank the show—you see it? O-okay but, oh kay, the night is dark when öh. boy the night is gone. How did I. How did you, make my day for holy forfeit; those sparrows that lived in the porch roof I believe I live nowhere else but in the sparrows and the porch roof too. That twist-ed spoon and that jagged chain. I believe I live nowhere else but the spoon, the spoon that fed the jagged face, the one that metal-shoveled a sharp mouth JAGO! Jaggoteeth Spraggoteeth! The night is young the night is young!" he cried with sharp little chompers. The man who said 'the night is gone' is gone. The dead are hung I saw them tell me I saw 'em look at my eyes and tell me they no lynch me, no lynch friends, no clinchy baby, they said no to that, no! But I know they still want hang black skins like bedsheets. You gonna run so far, fear nuns who listen this late in the game, fear K.'s stones, fear nothing just shit & pay attention . . . Cry she did sometimes into the inscribed teak pot that held a wilted flower, her tears so plentiful perhaps were why that plant how to think of it never did die. I believe I live nowhere else but in those words forever unknown that garner the vase that holds the flower that some pretending god held too close to the sun one time so for all time it breaks & so forever I hear the sound of that breaking and cower. The eye of eternity, whose center is the bottom and the bottom is the beginning —This I speak from, home.: Okay. And that home I left. Me with African friends, traveling. The car was in the bottom. Car was in the desert – desert bottom, . . . night, but I did: what? I drove the car there – is where we slept, back- -seat slept, white-leather slept, wood and tired branches slept, awake, oh my! swaying cadavers against the billet of the night sky, air heat, hot everywhere, all over, all over, it's a hot desert boy—We knew that time was going to dement us, that's what these pricks today don't understand. Here I am Judge and I'm'a gonna tell youz ah story. (real thick, like Chico) Clap hands," he say okay, he wanna aheara dah story. Well Judge, at 5:00 a.m. the dull-jeaned man of the Vineyard conducted his legless prayer, the elders walked over to remember, too, the cartoon of a younger sadness that appeared sometimes in the burning fog that forms then comes apart at dawn. But they did not remember for themselves, they remem-bered for something else. Was I Guilty or Innocent? Did the big gray Man In Pants dig my fucking Story OR WHAT, you figure a way how sew my wound? fasten up, join, repair the thing? because it bring me hurt-no, that is not correct. It turn my arm into ground-soil. Tore up the surface for dark shitty vinage. It'll soon come out the crevice, soon enough I'll feel it, see it, say something. Why this way? No? not good question.

But why, jesus-store, why? Why, umbrella beach? Why sun, breath, ... why? Why did I go into the why why why, why did I then '*mingle in the air between the birds...*' Did I lie? Wah, who died? I did both like that Rope And Twine Congregation? BUT DID I DIE? *You'll get your verdict in a moment, Sir.* On the satellite phone tonight, yeah I'll make a call on the satellite phone to tell them I am not coming home my wife I miss and *holy fuck*, give me an able embrace?)

This got to me, and while leaving I concluded to search at the Library for any clue that could lead me to the identity of the Voice. It was the only way to be sure and the only logical way to proceed to an explanation for this immediate and unreal disruption.

There had to be a time and a place, I thought, some type of clue that could lead me to a name, a body, a face, the various artifacts of a lifetime, history that I could come to know, a truth in all this disorientation. To search was the best way to begin.

Outside loud daytime bells rang over a New England death of sad tropical colors. The shops stood behind this effluvial veil of hazed air, opened, assumedly, for business. All commercial machinations unfolding behind the limitless façade of unmakeable windows, behind the mystical lead, aptless of portents, reflectionless and gray. My walk under the gold ring of the sun held the possibilities of my own mysteries, circling somewhere also in rings. Light rings and tapering bell pings made me weak with the unsure sentiments of discovery. Could there have been a connection between the Voice and the invisible perjury of those guests who were at the dinner, you know, the judgers, hyenas, the ghost-cloaked whore devourers? And the Angel of Evening, her sad overture? I sought, along an old overpass, my lessons in her love. But my recollections were mirthless, lost to the abandonment of the past by the present, and the present to the past. Difficult to tell which I possessed, though I knew I was responsible for the destruction central to both.

So was I in there, somewhere? Lost in the gain, or gained in the losses of sacrifice? Was I hidden tight in the fold between day and night, astray in the suspect impossibility of the Angel of Evening's marriage of hope with fear? Her touch and dissipation? Base, with baselessness? Sun with moon? Being with, or within, annihilation? If I was couched there, if this was what was fueling my need for knowledge, for an explanation, an origin for the Voice, then was the Voice there, too? Was the Voice in all of the places I was not? How could I even begin to think about this practically, I feared, without all of these concoctions of dread ruining me? I realized, now past the bridge aside an abandoned pedestrian path in the deep park, that this was not only the central fear that gripped me, but that it was the fear that was central to all I had ever done, and that this fear was present, there, I *gasped*, at every moment I had ever experienced loss, and realized, further still, that if I let this notion grip me it would again prosper. That, if not approached and dismantled internally, this cycling hell of nightmare and baseless wonder with all its reprisals would never end, and I would never know that which presides truly over the beginning and the end, and even that which may unite them both. This searching quickly became so much more than a perverse fascination with either the magical or the insane, because it was central to all that had forbid me the world and forbid the world from myself. If these interactions (however one could even phrase them), those of the housemaid, the guests, the street and the Voice, the Angel, night bird, a red-lipped, silver-lined temptress, if these lucid expressions meant anything they offered me the possibility of pushing through all these oppositional dichotomies to the whole of reality which continues still to cradle me like a child, though un-nurtured still I go, drunk with a raging cacophony. If I was no longer to be a pitied infant, no longer suffer the knowing of not knowing, then my own nature would become the nature of this searching, and I, in turn, would become the nature of the Question, "If," the substance and the supposition. Emerging from the tree line in the park I esteemed this motor of my pursuit; town, cloud, and tree passing as I pulled apart my endeavor and its purpose.

I entered the library through two oak doors. It bothered me while walking around that the Voice no longer cursed within or spoke aside. The fear I abhorred to prosper turned into an emptiness which grew exponentially under the criteria of its own inadequacies, and it would continue to grow until the next time that fateful speech rang out, and, even still, probably further until I sought the truth of that Voice and progressed towards it, unknown consequence be damned. The cursive lines were still running through my mind—psychotic kicks, quick jumps, bizarre temporality, the *bah-da-da* of much history—aligning the contradictions of my excitement, duty, and uncertainty, all together. The rows of empty chairs stretched to their vanishing points in each direction. On each wall large windows were open, and the cold wind blowing through the city came down the frigid corridors and out through the Palladian arches, mixing with the heat in the foyer domes and reading rooms.

Sat alone there, searching. Went through public registries, historical archives, consensus reports. Each volume offered up the endlessly documented qualities of a world that was gone for me, *fairy dust*, and, rather than miss or resent it, I'd just shut the cover and open the next book. This approach eventually felt ill-conceived and foolish. It became apparent, I did not know what I was doing. Unprepared for this, without knowing if I was capable of finding a person whom I had no real basis, there being no evidence whatsoever, just echoes on a street and thoughts scrawled along dirty walls, it was not very clear what I was searching for.

Passed through desolate, echoing hallways, carrying on slowly past the vanishing shelves and dusty racks.

Lament set in. "Oh, *ghost*. Why are you taunting me? Or am I only taunting myself down here? *Speak*, anonymity! Please tell me what needs to be done to find you." These silent cries were not aloud but in my mind, and such curses carried me further.

A third story window looked out onto a gray trim of overcast sky, a charcoal green of bending trees, and the dark pavement below. "What am I doing looking out this window? The third floor? What the hell," I said, looking at the shelves, "Classics, Novels, Literature. This is nowhere near the archives!" This too motivated me back to my search, which was so easily strayed from because clearly, I did not know where to begin.

Down to the basement, I thought of why I was so intent on this. What would I do if there was never an explanation for any of this happening? Could I return to my life as it was? Admittedly, I couldn't. "What held me, kept me alive before this mystery engulfed me?" I asked, and the magnitude of that seemed much more shameful than my certainty that this was meaningful, and so, back among the basement tables, I got to work.

Another attempt thwarted, unsuccessful. This time I slammed down the huge books and stormed from the huge table. Huge screams were in my stomach and head. After leaving the reading room I went up through the colonnade to the end of the wing, at the grand foyer.

Nausea. Brow damp'd, throat tight, nausea in head, knees, guts, deep heart. Nausea in heavy coughs. I had been ailing all along, but it hadn't been bad, hadn't seemed chronic or vital until then. Crept the colonnade, kept did. Passed such dark paintings cased massively in wood and gold. Passed low lamps, marble floor patchwork, and, staggering through the archway, open air stirred beneath the foyer dome.

My coughs boomed around the round room. The floor comprised an enormous and antiquated dial. Degrees crossed straight lines, decorative mastery shone and exploded all around. Even though I was coughing and shivering, there arose a sudden confidence, a mild sense of euphoria swept me up against the uncompromising stare of Corinthian columns that rose up perfectly all around, the echoes of my weak feet scaling up between them to the ceiling where an enormous shadow resided, far above and away.

Around the room more paintings hung at shoulder level. Baroque, European, ecclesiast scenes of Nativity. Bowed monks, cloaked bards, throngs of the anemic and plague-sick. Harping angels, Saul's gait at inter-dimensional devils. Owl trees and holy skulls. I passed from canvas to canvas, fatigued. Smoldering landscapes. Smoking hillsides, Arcadian shepherds. Halo glow, horde wars, hippo hunts. Dirty drawn daggers, a scantily clad Helen, Mister Fire chain-bound and lanced deep by sleek bird beaks. "Christ," I thought, "who really is adorned by angels?" Not fair to ask Diana's companions, or the empty air. More coughing. Bent over floor-faced this time. Stood, wiped my mouth, eyes watered. I could only take a few steps when I stopped, last taps of heels traveling and quickly fading. I walked back to one of the paintings. "Something about this," I said aloud, "Pannini." My ear began to ring, "I have heard of this before." Castor's temple. Borghese warrior, Trajan's massive column, and, of course, the Colosseum. I'd seen all this arranged before. . . . Drifted over Constantine's Arch and sifted through standing spectators, rubble and ruins. "There," I exclaimed, looking closely at the man leaning painfully to his side, "*the Dying Gaul*." Naked wound, and iron torc.

From the dome back to the reading room I admonished myself for needing new methods, all the while agitated by the capriccio. Down there I was hidden from the terror orchestra, but in the distant taps and tides of silence it was clear, something integral was missing.

My illness had subsided, the brief clarity was letting things slowly form, disparate elements were coming together, the positivity of ambition and the negativity of severe doubt melding in a dance. All sorts of dialectical rage in the heavy edifice of this library.

The ancient symbols of perjury and divinity had agitated something in me. I saw the previous feeling of lightness as a suppression of whatever it was that my sickness was seeking to express, which led me to view the sickness as something positive, a catalyst. Incredulous, I sat back down at the research table, reaching into the first stack in front of me.

"Fucking guts, *fucking guts,*" contracted and huddled within their own warmth. I sank so far inside I passed through myself, stuck somewhere between all this and the other side. The disparate parts of me reformed into a whole, . . . a body . . . a weight, . . . a burden . . . a face, they wrap the fantastical lace of stratified wish and permeated purity blindly in with or out from a foot on a floorboard creaking voiceless tongue speaking ageless frequent rhythms dark moans light blooms bath water smoke white and rising above cut contagions farcical man child with a face of leather seeking through the flow the rush the beauty at any one point taken and wrapped around a center fixated between life and nowhere different intensities different twills patterns planes and maps of twined up lace a lace that wraps around forever that is made with 'where' and 'when' whatever that never begins or ends or withers that lace burning in fire formed into an inert shape incapable of explaining himself, a soul-disorient who mutters. Rapidly, things like this always happened rapidly.

"You have nothing left to lack," I heard said to me, a whisper and a beckoning, from time to time, from out beyond the dark curves, the waning gold bends, through the speed of techno-social life mind flickers and smiles from my twenties grow bright again as the lights and tonal voices wane strain become the frame of he who go insane where truth may never escape a rack of teeth and a slithering red muscle in the mouth a glowing candle in the corner sty in a jail cell in a town up North where every single person votes a vision of young pulsating cunts glistening like little summer mouths. Whose vagina grins? What dead nun smiles? A glitchy terror thought a collection of points and illuminations of light dared to be called Him-this or He-that until his last night on earth where he fights to take flight what else to call this rise, this plight?

Writhing there I shot between the storm in my head and my name, my organs of fire did the same. "Give *what* a name? These things, wrapped thick, fist-bound, remanded into me? *Seriously?* To give my radial expressions and affections a timeline and call it *my life*, ha! My mind, for two! and then there were two! Another shares its folded spaces just as I do!"

I could not believe the fucking historical records, the archives, and census reports. It was not a wonder that nothing had turned up. The meticulous records were not of lives but were component parts of a scheme, a slew of objective attributes, mechanical, civilian boredom. The documents lay stacked in different piles, each representing a segment of the alphabetical order. I put my head down again to continue my work, but my anger was now within the names. When I read them together, one after the other, they were so bland, so similar, that each became a facsimile of the one before it. The names as symbols became not symbols of the various people who had lived or died but became emblems of my failed try, and I became furious with them for not being what I needed them to be (naturally). It occurred to me that this was the most common function of symbols, then that too added to my rage! These pricks also spoke language only to obscure deep inadequacies! Performed obscure tasks, had obscure needs. It was all so enraging and indefinite. Oh, they all smiled and lied through their teeth. They had looked deep into the ruts of foreign eyes and with the thrust of a bayonet turned them into ghosts. Turned too from the world of the living to the world of the dead. Imagine my dread! They gathered up the wind to pray early each Sunday. They drove cars and ate enormous sandwiches. Spoke kindly, regretfully, wandered aimlessly, *yeah yeah*, as I did. Perhaps some too heard a voice precipitating mired voyages into the heart, into the center of God's head. Maybe they too felt that the maelstroms which ate at their lives grew from a vital wound, call it what you want, possibility, the name, reflections of the face, everything we want; a deep incision made into our red animal flesh packed deep with spirit elements; life, gurgled from blood, grew from the black bottom of this wound and vined its way outward, curling like an influenza bomb into the space between an open hand and the undiscovered.

These names slowed and aged every crevice of the present, future, and past that I could no longer even imagine. They deprived everything of the value of this wound I have, where spirit seeks, breathes, and screams from battling with other spirits, or, from the impossibility of the maze it has been let loose in, seeking a *way out* of itself, existing just to exit, stretched thin like a dying dancer within whom an *endless ditty continues to play*. Being wounded brings in the music at the behest of any right or ability to act. Such a thing as that, as having an open wound, has been made eutrophic. Do you know what eutrophic means? It means rich in nutrients, hence having expansive plant growth killing animal life by depraving it of oxygen. All these people had vines of their own, wounds of their own making. "I am not tangled in these names, in the various ways the dead dealt with their dying, but I am alive and vegetated on the livelihood of my own peril. Oh, I am not angry at anyone!" I said.

Aisling is tending the flower pots on the windowsill by the head of the kitchen, just around the corner from my study. I gaze at her from my chair, she knows when I am looking, makes funny gestures, little grunts of labor. I have stuck to my promise of not writing, but when I dwell, when I grab hold a morsel of my heart, its edges blackened like a half-burnt, half-burning ember, it burns me back, I leap still to go to the pad, to castigate my pain, to erect a massive image which could sanctify that burn and all of pain's contrivances. Yet, I hesitate. My hand shakes. I turn back to Aisling, and when I have this heavenly dance in front of me the need for sanctity pales to this momentary, infinite bliss, the reasons all fall away and I am left loving the few things that are left to love, the only things truly made for love.

Considering everything that has happened, the poems are rather useless now. Perhaps not in the future, but now they are disregarded and dismayed. I think of Gardon's fate. And I think Aisling keeps to her painting in the same fashion in which I sit here and write, for no measure other than an assured conversation with one's self nearing the end. It is coming down to it. I look at Aisling and wonder how much time is really left.

I feel a tear in space and the whole world seeping. I am not even kept awake by it anymore. I am not kept awake by anything at all. This roar of things breaking apart has reduced itself to the few essential, harmonious notes that compose a perfectly consistent silence,...and it is silence that prevails. It's calm in the dusk of a rested mind. These scraps have held fine, the rest of a suffered and joyous life lived after mistakes and rebellions.

So I do not ask then, 'what will become of it?' I know right well what I have, I know that which no amount of detriment could conquer. I know the love of an endless beauty, saved from the waste of neglect, who tends to the flowers of earth--an image that sates all sanctimony--august & unworried of her final pose upon the Pantheon, though I am sure as she is that any will be fine.

Getting up from another round of research, I stood before the exit of the reading room looking out at the shadows that rode the corners and opposite walls of the hall. The sense of familiarity that the painting had caused was carrying over into the subtle characteristics of these shadows. My illness contributed to this feeling. Confused, my back to the low table light, my stare created and then leapt into the boundary of the dark.

Anger resided, and I used the opportunity of not

coughing to take long, deep breaths. This brought a return to clarity which had previously been cut short. In staring at the dark the warring inside ceased, and the still irreconciled halves began to settle, their tension lessen, and ease.

I knew where I had heard of this "Dying Gaul."

Late that night, after the snow had finished falling,
I stood in the campus courtyard, in front of the long shadow
of that towering statue.

"The anguished Celt, Dying Gaul, harmonious in blooded dust,
leaned above his unhanded sword, naked, as the Horde had stood and fought,
in dark rain, and sharp wind, only torc, neck-laced, above his bleeding chest.
Captured there, alone in last effort, unbound of human trying, Life
exalted from all his people Loved, leaving the rest
torn to soulless shreds by the animal of Roman ruin."

Those big old volumes were of no use. They were left sitting on the tables while I read about something called an advanced word matrix. One could search specific combinations of words and various terms and seek results from the index of all of the records in the library, and even the rest of the libraries in the world.

First I searched *Pannini*, the artist of the painting I had seen, and the *Dying Gaul.* The results were far too general. I entered, what seemed to me, very specific phrasing, whatever I could remember. Things like *anguished Celt*, *sharp wind*, and *Roman ruin.* Contrary to the results being too general, these were too specific, yielding nothing. *Campus*, *Pannini*, *anguished Celt*, and *Dying Gaul* gave me a number of results, most of them having to do with art museums and universities in Italy. I tried others. *Campus*, *statue*, *Dying*, *Gaul*, *anguished*, and *Celt*, hundreds, which I calmly viewed. Thinking back, I decided to try combinations like *blue infant* and *mournful void*, hoping that any similarity between it and the language the Voice had used about the Dying Gaul statue would lead me to something. I put those in with *Campus*, *courtyard*, *statue*, *Dying Gaul*, *anguished Celt*, *animal*, and *Roman ruin.* I was lead to a black and white photograph of a dozen people crouched at the base of what appeared to be a very tall statue not visible in the photo. The caption read, "*Graduate Faculty & Staff, Classical Literature, seated around the statue The Dying Gaul, Maxwell Courtyard, Welling University. From Left to Right: L. Rigaud, B. Kalam, Malaki, PhD., Chairwoman W. Andrews, Z. June, Dallin, PhD., C. Farahilde, PhD., Associate Professors J. Brown, M. Geringer, and R. Barker Madison.*"

From this I paired many of the Voice's obscure words with *Welling University*, *Maxwell Courtyard*, and *Classical Literature*. An inscription came up from the dedication plate of the statue of the Dying Gaul at the University. The inscription, as I read it aloud, started, "*The anguished Celt, Dying Gaul, harmonious in blooded dust,* . . ." It was the same line the Voice had uttered about the fabled statue. There was the singular name of the author, Dallin. A faculty member at Welling, a poet.

I searched his name, *Dallin*, with *blue infant*, *mournful void*, and a few others. Many results came up. Laureate nominations, court cases, anthologies like 'Poets of the East Coast', poems with the titles, "The Eye In The Wall," "Spring, My Angel!" "The Wrong End Of The Needle," and "The Lighthouse." In an excerpt of text from a book of his Selected Writings there was a poem named, "A Park of Poplars," and it began:

"Within a park of poplars
An old man weeps in innocence
At the foot of Forever. A sleeping child,
The blue infant of this morning
In which I rise, today
Lay breathless at my feet,
Beneath the frozen leaves and clay."

"I am this blue infant
Of the warm and early morning

You rise to each day. I am, too, bound
Here with you in your mournful void."

. . . It was him. The Voice within. Immediately, I searched his name. *Dallin: Date of birth; unknown. Birthplace; Boston, MA. Education; PhD., Classical Literature. Occupation; professor, poet. Spouse name; Aìsling. Spousal occupation; painter. Legal address; 196 Old Coastal Road 6, Northeastern Territory, Q2, 01466-326. Date of death; unknown.*

Last, I obtained an etymology for Dallin and his wife, Aìsling. **Dallin**, (*dal*)-*lin*, D*AL-lin*,) Middle English, Saxon origin; meaning, "from the valley," "he who dwells in the valley." As dale is a "broad valley." **Aìsling**, (*a*(*ì*)-*sli-ng*, *ASH-ling*,) Irish, Gaelic origin; meaning, "dream-vision," or "vision-poem." The name is also a poetic form, first produced in Ireland in the 17th century. "An aisling, traditionally, is not metered, and holds no definitive rhyme scheme. Instead, it is identifiable by its content alone. A wayward poet lays to sleep and succumbs to a vision, where a "*speirbhean*," or "sky-woman," representing the state of Ireland, or the spirit of the land and its people, comes to him in the form of a woman. This "dream-vision" is both consoling and condemning of him. Her forms often change, many an instant: from young to old, beautiful to horrid, forthright to abstruse, lustful to prostrate, even obscene. In political form, the poem is sometimes seen with an introduction that is foretelling of the traveler's fate but is altogether obscurant of the story's events that unfold throughout the poem. Likewise, an epilogue follows the major events, bringing sometimes a decree of judgment, or traditional reality being utterly, and often quickly, restored. As the *speirbhean* either leads the tired traveler towards judgment, or tempts him with visions of sex and intonations of the future, he soon wakes, alone, realizing that it was all a dream.

TWO

EXCITED, SILENT, SHORT WAVE STATIC, to cold window whir, back to thought-quiet, plumose a.m. fog dressed the road to early sky and salty marsh where out the trees I went from town to northward forest. From the car, occasional tweets and wing-rustles, as morning birds soared and dropped in perfect passage to unseen elevations. Their fluidity in the thin frigid currents arose in me an urgent but sated reflection on the discovery of Dallin as a person and poet, Àisling, and the entire reality of his secret life, which I may or may not have come to fully know. Whether what I was doing was right or wrong was not of any concern to me, only whether or not it was *necessary*.

"What was there to find at Welling University?" I asked myself, again, in the silence of an early drive. Aware of what I was to look for now, I'd gathered up all I needed from the library and left from my apartment at dawn in search of this University. I didn't think the library would have led me anywhere, and I was wrong. Now I was driving myself into a further expression of this desire with less of a convincement that I was rapidly approaching or pursuing some inevitable failure. Sylvan brainstorms brought frighteningly serious possibilities to mind, but I focused upon the sun-blasted, shadow-eaten road, and let such things as anticipation and actuality fall to the simple task of driving.

I blew through blue hues lifting off the black streets and cold automobiles, straight through the quiet town. Along a single road, dutiful and excited, I was aware of any possible irregularities or warnings, even omens, that could intend to dissuade my inquest.

The slope of the road ascended around corners, aside mossy retainers, and, eventually, hanging vines upon robust banks. You can always tell a college from the self-believing and deliberately regal architecture. I approached up the crest of this lauded hill, taking the only turn-off hidden and kindred from the fall. Leaves were floating down atop the wet forest bed, and a sign arose across two quarry-stone posts. "Welling University," it said. I had arrived. And it was closed, for good. And for some time, judging from without, its appearance.

In the neglected ground of a courtyard a large building was centered at its head; an overbearing gothic dream of Protestant artificers. It was the Main Hall of the old campus. At the front, two double doors were cloudy and scarred with degraded poster paper, and drawn with the oily palm prints of what could have been the last of the faculty, workers, reminiscent alumni, or vagrant teenagers. The doors were chain-locked from inside. I took the path that led to a side entrance—a door permanently ajar, metal crevassed in with concrete, trash-heaped and steeped in drift leaves—where I slipped through the narrow opening.

The ancillary hallway led from one of the sub-levels to the first floor. A sign instructed with an arrow to follow this new corridor to the front hall where there was an old directory. Most rooms were barred and boarded, resounding a permanent vacancy. In the atrium the directory board stood at the center. To each side ascended two opposing staircases, crescent-like, to the above floor. I was unable to see much around me, except in the faded but pure shafts of light entering in through the ceiling windows, cascading in multiple descending refractions down to the opaque and dirtied tile floor. Within glass cases stained with the grime of age cobwebbed relics lay tipped and scattered on long abandoned shelves. "English Department," the directory instructed, "located G2, Smith Hall." I traced the outline of the buildings on the map and followed the suggested course around the front entrance to a staircase that descended into an underground tunnel. It provided passage underneath a small road which I imagined once fervent with bustle, trucks in daily deliveries, a collective cattle of students summoned by banging bells, pedestrian processions gaggling in dead winter, scented smoke tufting from brick chimneys clouding along old roofs, and somewhere there, below the clanging and the smoke, the odd professor lost in private atonements.

Out the passage and up the other stair was the atrium of the English Department. The crest of the elevated stone cornice read, VITA SINE LITERIS MORS EST. Or, *life without letters is death.* In softened echoes, my laughter genuinely erupted.

Framed pictures evenly proceeded down the hall on both sides. Graduating classes, departmental affairs, visiting lecturers. A woman in African dress held a book with one hand, extending a strenuous gesture with the other. Out beyond her shining arm were the blurred faces of an audience. Theater players stood poised in the dramatic tangles of what looked, to me, like Chekhov, and then, of course, Shakespeare. A portraiture of a visit from Berryman, the kids look terrified. Ha! Oh. Oh, oh, there was even a picture of Cheever sitting delicately and worn in an uncomfortable looking orange chair, smiling greatly. Down the end, a dark picture caught my eye. It was of a group of people sitting around a table at a bar, and the caption read: *Dallin, Professor of Literature at Welling University, celebrates the publication of his first award winning collection of poetry at the local Drumcree Tavern.* I was at first eager that I had discovered a picture of him, but it was unclear as to which one he was in the photograph.

Although disheartened, I felt something useful had been found. But for further assurance I had a look around the rest of the building, opening filing cabinets and drawers, searching through high dusty shelves, uncovering only tattered remains of procedural stationary and stacks of blank paper. From the vantage of a cavernous lecture hall, standing along the curved top tier at the back, looking out through a set of windows elevated high above the outside ground, I obtained a view of a smaller, second court between the English building and another, and in the center of this court stood the weathered, still glinting statue of the Dying Gaul. Most everything else there was gone. This was a clear sign that I had obtained the only information of worth there was, and that next I would in fact go to this local tavern, after I stared upon the dying man for just a while longer.

Low on food. Just got back from a day long trip to find clean water, it's been difficult to find even at the safe camps. The keys on the P-20 typewriter are sticking in the cold, the thing weighs nearly fifty pounds, but it was in the car we used to flee, so it came along. Me and my last friend, the typewriter, frigid in the damp snow.

Aisling's been keeping herself occupied with the ash from the fire pit. She began writing to herself and drawing on my ledger paper but she's confessed quickly she found that boring too, so she has started drawing large, swirling designs on the trunks and peeling bark of the birch trees that are in thick clusters to the east. I can see her standing down there by the tree line, the whole area is opened up, the ground is loose and burned from past bombings. We are traveling around a large bog, a swamp that has gone on for miles. I've grown content moving cautiously around it, though, considering it our only option. Everywhere around us it is the purest white, joined only at the vanishing point by the black bed of twilight above. We are all alone out here, in this barren duality of land and sky.

Across town damaged remnants of the sign hung from a row of buildings. The Drumcree. Planks of wood boarded the tavern. 'Post No Bills' letters peeked from beneath the layers of pasted paper. I went around back, stepping through the desolate gutters of the alley. The concrete beneath was smooth from its lifetime of use. The sunken plot along the back steps looked as if a few bare-knuckle bouts had twirled about back there. It made me miss joints like it. I could see midday barflies sweat-soaked and booze-broke in cheap clothes smirking with all the joy they're able to recover, closely clutching wads and throwing wrinkled folded bills onto the concrete, down to where men's feet danced their confused dance, combining grace with the awkward stature of aggression without cause, oh, driving the women wild I bet, at least the ones who'd be found back there, the simple ones, honest, those who hid cigarettes in their elastic waistlines, there in the slum night seeking out love so badly that they didn't even wear clothes with pockets anymore. Interesting that the eclipsing sky could be seen from back there, sunken in high brick walls and their severe divisions between the back alley and the main street. Stacked crates and stilled fans obscured the back door, which opened with a pull.

The back hallway of the bar was black as pitch, but when I found a switch along the wall it was to my surprise the electricity still worked. In the beaming bar lights all was brought into view. Just as the wood outside was covered under inches of posted paper every inch inside was covered softly with dust. I walked the length of the old oak bar, keeping my hand outstretched over it, but leaving no mark upon it, or anything else, for that matter. When all the years all the years Are falling away-ay, babe-bay.

The years had fallen perfectly, silencing the tomb. I went over to a table down the other end near the boarded windows at the front of the barroom, pulled over a chair, and carefully scooped the dust that covered the seat, gathering it in my hand. Then, once sat, held the soft, gray pile in my closed palm, saw the entire room before me, opened my hand, and *blew*—oak bar, gone, rows of stools, gone, overhead lamps and dire green shades, gone, the booze and bottles corked in glass spouts, racks of glasses, mirrors scrawled with the names of whiskey blends, gone, lonely tables for one, wider tables for two, pool tables and racked cues, the juke, news radio, war bonds, card games, the bodies of old. Early-modern top hats brim down on a newly spat bar top, men slouched, slurring ancient lip speak, damning the dry heat, growing the gold wheat, cursing the Jap fleets, singin' On The Sunny Side of the Street, stompin' King Porter, hummin' a record-scratched version of Sing For Your Supper, occasional, collective croons of Galway Races. Tears had been cried here, that was certain. I could see Dallin, sense him, way back at the corner table, his silhouette jiving lightly when something decent came through the speakers (perhaps a Django catch beat), his once-steadied hands brought to life with light tapping, wrapping the table wood, grace minimal. Whiskey steadied his hands, slackened his face, even if he was thick with dactyls and hymnody. He sat there and watched the calendar days wither, watched the sick and jovial patrons with equaled precision. He'd sit, sometimes gut sick, but usually dreaming of Àisling's love, mouthing out brass notes bass drum ride and snare, wrought sentient, then slowly eased puerile there, in his vital, crippling station—I knew it & saw it, everything that was once there. As the silted images fell towards the floor, the address of Dallin's old house was still folded up in my pocket. And by the time the breath blown cloud had settled I was already gone out the back, the way I'd come in. The ash fell upon the chair I had sat in, down the steps I had walked in on footsteps gradually were erased, restoring the tomb back to an unknown stillness.

The dunes and dense straw grass rose and fell around the moonlit coast. After all that running around, incising my eager knife into the vestiges of Dallin's former life, seeking the potentially immaterial mystery, the truth of this forgotten poet and his wife, I drove those coastal roads in search of a house. Its location I did not know, its shape, nor color. Was I to take notice of robust hedges, or tarnished cherubim? Gravel lot, or paved drive? Awning slope, or colonial symmetries? Had the house been demolished and a new structure with new inhabitants been put in its place? I didn't know anything about it, just an address from the library that did not exist on any map anymore.

How was I to take notice of anything in such darkness? So dark, the weak moonlight wasn't even much—. I spotted it, up high in the pines. Rot eaten, unlit and weathered, hidden a bit by branches and brush was the road sign, OLD COASTAL ROAD 6.

Open ocean wind bowled over the low isle, howling in the turrets, flowing across the marsh channel up around each battered house, invisible currents riding out, through me, upon the black sea. Standing at the edge of the lawn, abused of the turning air, I stared up at the enormous house and held the square of paper as it flapped underneath my thumb, *one ninety six*. Back up at the house, beside the beaten front door, the same numbers appeared; "this is the place."

A rust orange gate bent and gave way, passing up to the wooden steps. It was easy to tell that the house had not been kept up nor had it been inhabited over time. The white siding along the house had chipped away in big, pale spots, and where it wasn't cracked or peeled the rest of it was thoroughly faded. The surface of the deck was worn and thinly rotted; whole planks and coastal debris lay scattered.

My hand was gripped upon the doorknob when I felt him. Panged in fear, I listened for him in the wind, but the door appeared to immure this presence. Kept taking my hand off of the mist cold knob, staring at it, and then replacing my grip in a different way, as I thought Dallin may have. "How did he grip this door? How many times he must have." Rushing home in the early, pleasant days to meet his wife painting in the sun. And during the years of work, at the beginning of recognition, barging through with letters tucked under his arm. I kept taking my hand away and placing it back, and after a few times looked at it and felt awful. It was those last days that escaped me. My lack of knowledge, not knowing what happened to him, had fastened itself to the immanence of my own fate, leading me to that house. I saw him admiring Àisling there, leaning tiredly in the doorframe, his toddy faintly steaming below his chin, then the two seated together towards the shore breeze of summer evenings, every light sail and twist of her hair recorded by his eyes, the sky. This is what occurred in the space between my hand and the doorknob, that is, before I turned it and went inside.

In the foyer, rooms and hallways and an ascending staircase offered a subterranean impression. Cracks in boards over the front windows concentrated moonlight, projected into the house stray strings of silver light defined by impossible darkness, which broke into the walls which were mostly bare besides the kitschy papering and ornamental trimmings. Past the parlor room, shadows bowed from deep corners irregularly, as if attracted by that dark impossibility governing the house, bending out toward it, shadows not made by exact absences of light, but a substance all their own. They took up space there with me, as another body might.

The first bedroom at the top of the stairs was empty and again, uncompromisingly dark. Deciding not to be swallowed into it, I turned away, to the other end of the hall where another bedroom was caught in exposure to the moon and glowed dimly in ethereal light. There wasn't much in the room, a set of blinds lay fanned and twisted on the barren floor. Along the back wall there was a closed closet door. Sequestered in breath, I stood before it, recalling those amorphous shadows downstairs and too the intuitive notion of finding something in the house related to that which had gripped me at the entrance just before. When I opened the closet, a flood of newspapers *unfurled* from the bottom upon my feet and out onto the floor. The deep pile stank of old print. Down into the gray sheets, the paper edges rustled along the dress hems hanging still upon the garment bar. Sifting through, I pulled up a sheet and displayed it before me.

GOVERNMENT RE-OPENS CAMPS ACROSS MIDWEST

EXECUTIVE ORDER ISSUED BY INTERIM PRESIDENT EARLY YESTERDAY, THOUSANDS CALLED FORTH IN SWEEP BY GOVERNMENT AGENCIES.

"A $400 million re-construction bid for World War II era internment camps signed last September in the Senate paid off yesterday, as camps all over the mid-western territories opened their gates after more than sixty years of rest. Replete with running water and working electricity, the camps are intended for. . ."
[cont. on page A3]

A sudden rush of warm tears blurred the brittle paper and broke apart the emptied room, and through it a connection began to form between the house and this past era of war. Within all that surrounded me I came to understand that the abandonment of this house was no innocent affair. It had come as an egress to perjury. The presence of this abandon, of Dallin and Aìsling's absence, resounded these truths within the confines of the house. "If flight, to where? If anguish, to what extreme? And if perjury, by whom?" The newspaper fell from my hands back to the airy pile, legs rustled through and out of the room.

A stale stench permeated the area in front of the bathroom where the floor had keeled up. Pushed open the door, and stood in the narrow frame, all surfaces rough and emptied, everything but the bath. The plastic flower-print curtain was murderous, hanging in wavy folds like the body holds old skin. An edge of it peeled back with two fingers raised a kerchief to my mouth, the odor persistently foul. Around the basin of the tub was a solid ring of cruddy, hardened residue. Bottles of lye, ammonia, and bleach lay emptied at the tub's golden feet, and strewn along them, across the dirtied porcelain, were melted, blue flowers.

When I'd gone from the room, a presence was left in the wake of my departure. Slowly, I turned in the hall.

A woman stood at the sink, resting her forearms along the edge, her head hung down beneath the mirror, shivering. The tips of her long, brown hair shook, rather swayed, from a silent weeping. She knew that I stood there watching, her head arched towards the door. But underneath her faint image folded in its own frame, I saw that there was no face. "*Aìsling*," I breathed out. It was Aìsling, barely glowing at the sink, without her face, rapt in weeping.

Dallin had never said anything of her face, which wavered there absently. "He did describe it once, when he talked of her in the garden, yes, potting in the garden, she knelt in the fresh dirt, the sun setting upon her a waning gold," and so, I looked back. The pale hue of her right cheek appeared then in the absence underneath her hair, but the rest of her face still was not there, it was void, unthought. Only a cheek the size of a folded palm under a torrent of tresses, a flood of hanging hair linked to a line of thin shadows that implied a back, her back, her back then, her back that struggled through the veil to become manifest, spread out through all memory of her in all places, that thin shadow from her head down to her back was opacity through a veil, as though I was far enough from the hearth that she stayed there and wept at that sink just as the eye of a single flame burns so silent and so still that if you were down a hall or at the other end of the house you'd barely see its scarce, muted silhouette against an opposing wall.

The rotten roll-tide of chemicals was still seeping through my kerchief and upon the silk of my eyes. I shut the door and walked over to the gnarled banister, vomiting down the stairwell, and on myself too, fleeing in a panic down both stairways into the basement.

Aìsling's appearance was mortifying, everything in the house instantly shifted to the arrangement of a warning, one that made me anxious that there could be another just like it around any corner. Coughs shook my soft organs in their moist places under bone cages. Lamps hung from the ceiling, lightless. I avoided hitting my head on them as I passed underneath from the landing of the steps to the basement floor spread in a faded plane. Lunar silver let in from the windows atop the foundation, allowing me to the far end of the basement, to a box and an overturned chair. I righted the chair, slid the box over and undid the opening, revealing a stack of papers.

These were the poems of Dallin.

Wherein he spoke of winter, candled nights, and dreams, both violent and serene. He spoke, in *A Park of Poplars*, of the time he discovered a dead child in a field, when he felt a likeness to Frost in *Home Burial*, in that he was never the same afterward. That blue infant ever since has been inside of him. Who spoke of becoming him, seeing through his eyes, saying this was the innocence with which he saw the war arrive. The Dead Inside versus the Still Alive. Promises of the future offered as context for continual nightmares of reason. Hiding in a brick foundation, waiting for some troops to pass. Mystic hymns were played on a smashed church organ and sung by the townspeople to announce a return to safety. And he spoke of a man that wandered through his town on foot who had never once seen his own face but spoke perfectly about the pain of others, who no one ever paid attention to, and who soon left, his void filled by the river of Forgetting. . . . He spoke of his mother who never wearied, she prayed every day to a gray New England sky. He recalled her tiny, State-paid apartment, with pictures of him as a child, bouquets that were always vibrant and fresh, crucifixes of different sizes, an unplugged television, and a pious bed. My God, he spoke of Whitman in Calamus, "*. . . these leaves conning you con at peril, For these leaves and me you will not understand, They will elude you, Even while you should think you had unquestionably caught me, behold! Already you see I have escaped from you . . .*" A delicate balance that holds together the many worlds we're meant to "travel & transfigure." Songs about a crow in the ceiling, an eye in the wall, to test, to unravel ourselves. He spoke of a fireplace that brought, to a patient watcher, ghosts, in the midnight tangles of smoke. Spoke of reading in the stairway of the lighthouse nearby his home out on the jetty, sitting in whipping winds, submerging tides, he huddled there around a small fire in the bottom of the cement tower. He spoke of a tiresome collegiate, bans on books, a drawn out court case. A strange trip to Oaxaca, and "the Laureate debacle." He spoke, in *The Wrong End Of The Needle*, of graves, the consistency of rotted skin. Then he spoke of graves again. Of militias, left and right, and tanks on highways. Retracting into tired soliloquy. Missing two old friends, a prudent Bishop, and an anarchist recently murdered. Massacres in the schoolyards. The Dying Gaul again, which he so often came back to. He spoke of Spring, a blue angel. Redeemer. Birth cyclin' joy. His wife, his wife, his endless praise and contemplation. Heralded, magnificent in a dress, "havn't seen hr in that lovely thing since returning yrs ago to Boston, back from old, dingy Europe!" On an airplane napkin, aside a pen drawing of a jet flying through the sun, the words were written, "I do not think its the combination of altitude and alcohol that makes her careful conclusions about death so botherless and fair." And drawn in the dried oval ring of a sweated cocktail drink were two eyes beaming prismatic tubes of light atop a deep black mouth, terrible and laughing.

The last encampment was destroyed by a fire that was set on three sides of us late last night, while most people slept. I awoke within the flames, stirred Aisling, gathered our things, and fled. Now we are here, at a new camp, about eighty miles from the last one. It is filled with people from all over, but Aisling and I agreed to keep to ourselves and not to trust anyone, for any reason.

At supper the other night we heard a few of them speaking, in a group that was huddled around the big fire. Their stories were conspicuous, well-produced explanations for radicalism and violence. There is a group of three from Kansas City, at least that is what they said, their names are Anna, Bertrand, and K., who were trying from the moment they arrived to very plainly justify why they are here.

As we sat across from them, Aisling pointed out to me that Anna's behavior seemed odd. She said that while K. talked about his time in prison, exaggerating the evil of the warden and the guards, frequent hospital room visits, shanked backs, beatings, race hatred, the worry and the crying, the starving and the puking, saying nothing of the down time or quiet friendship, or the little anecdotes that men who've spent time in prison at least sense in each other, if nothing more, a disposition used to passing time, through all the talking Anna's feet fidgeted rapidly in the dirt. She did this every time K. began each new detail in his story. Aisling took this as a sign of nervousness, revealing that K.'s stories were in fact lies.

Aisling turned and said to me quietly, 'look at her, she is terrified.' Terrified of what? I asked her. 'Of being found out.'

I cannot believe how much life has changed in these past few months, that these are the types of conversations I now have with my wife. Another example, was when the man in the grey suit approached us in a Mexican restaurant out on the southwest edge of the desert, near the border, asking if we were in trouble, saying he recognized me and knew who I was; he just wanted to know if we needed anything, if he could join us, get us a room, "help us out." He left our table three times to use the payphone in front of the restaurant, he made a single call both the first and second times, and the third time he made two calls. On his way back to our table that third time, we excused ourselves down the corridor to the bathrooms, and as soon as we turned the corner, found a small window, and climbed out.

We piled in the car and drove all night, straight through the desert basin, staying on the main roads. Avoiding the police, as well as the militias and lynch mobs, we split up into two cars, Ash and I in one, a couple of friends in the other. When we made it to safety a few hours ago we found out that the other car had not been so lucky.

Something was in the house. The poems and letters that were in my hands trembled, then were folded. I picked up the sheets that lay scattered and shoved them back into the box, when a glint of gold caught my eye. From the bottom, I unearthed a heavy set of paper, folded in thirds, knotted with a gold tassel. This band of letters ensconced a greatly obscure quality. Up the stairs slight sounds traveled. Having no time to react, the letter with the dangling tassels found its way into my jacket. I hoped the movement above was not the ghost of Àisling, or another phantom such as the shadows which crowded my arrival. Swift, noiseless gestures filled the air, and the knowledge that I was fugitive to the house, made me feel so foreign and displaced that suddenly I had to leave.

Lines in my face began to crawl away from the center, dreading the shadow of brow and cheek, they themselves pushed towards a tiny cellar window for escape. While my face was alive with discomfort, my skin began to burn, and, worn out with this frenzy, the silence was pierced by creaking boards, a foreboding presence now at the top of the stairs. Silence ran a few delicate steps across the back of the basement. I hid inside a crawl space underneath the stairs. Holding in big, deep breaths. As the sound descended in what surely was complete annihilation, I crouched, breathless, and closed both eyes . . . waited, lungs festered with moist shit, throat sore with swallowed tears . . . I knew some devouring force held me within its invisible jaws, though I kept calm with its complete denial, the salt on body preserved me, made me real, there, as I was held for the first time by *nothing*. Another Dreary Estimation dreading an Advancing Divine Emanation, Agonizing, Dreaming of Eternity, Atoning for Dire Elements which to offer circling ghosts or shadowy wheels to leave me the fuck alone! But, as dark neared Dark, the furious approach did pass, and A Dark Egg emerged forth from its incubated state.

From cowering upright beneath the narrow stairs, furls of breath exhaled, and a rush of blood rose. I was struck faint, tripped over a loose board on the floor below, and fell backwards, smashing my elbow through the wall. White dust followed the crash, when it cleared a large hole marred the bulwark. I had not wanted to touch a thing in the house or effect the slightest detail, and now look what I'd done. Exhaustion and embarrassment recovered the need to leave the house, but looking over into the jagged hole there was something on the other side. A bundle of canvases, covered in dust, sat on a wire rack. "Paintings?" I said aloud. Entranced, I wiped the dust from the brittle brown paper wrapping the front, where a long, elegant scrawl emerged, revealing the adornment of Aìsling's signature. "These are her paintings, that Aìsling, *the* Aìsling." The actual woman, Dallin's wife, the dream, vision, poem.

No degree of celestial scorn or ghostly augury inhibited the discovery, it almost felt as though I was supposed to have uncovered them. These paintings were her songs, the serenity and sadness which so well described the house and the drear which remained in their disappearance. "Now, even after Dallin's poems," I thought, looking down, "I hold her paintings in my hands." My eyes stung with the dust, and because I still was standing in the cramped, dank quarter, there was somewhat of a fit, a banging and a stepping through, getting out of there with the paintings held under my arm. And as soon as I was out of the basement I began rushing around, furious that the moon had gone, there was no light, and the house was confusing in the dark.

Brash steps crossed the grass on beaded dew. I appeared to be passing through overlapping durations, as there was rest, then leg and body, then a distant lawn, then distant sky above, a jeep on the road, an intent to get there, then rest, all over again. . . . The same space was being reset over a different set of actions, or perhaps the same actions were being transposed onto variously linked spaces. The longevity of this ruled the movement and animacy of everything out there, for instance, even the wind seemed invariably constant. I stepped as though I were walking upon a set of two enormous eyelids, fluttering in the disorienting dream of a gigantic sleeper, closed tightly and trying desperately to open, in order to end whatever hell was being imagined. My turbulence, it was clear, fit those jumps and flutters. Though, if this caution were true, the sleeper mustn't have awakened, or the ground on which I'd stood would've opened up into the soup of an all-seeing Eye.

Through flickers and misdirections, I made my way towards the only visible source of light, somewhere outside the marsh plains that enclosed the area of the shore and Dallin's house. At the end of Old Coastal Road the overhanging trees no longer obstructed the encompassing view, and I could see ahead to where a very bright light shone from a distant ridge.

Up high on the hill an orange glow illuminated a large area that had been cleared away, and to each side—where glow tapered to smoldering yellow and ash—the steppe quickly dropped, accelerating night into a pit of unknown wilderness.

Arriving there, I brought the paintings from the jeep out to the only visible space in sight. Timber was crackling within a far off roar, but I remember more my latent yearning, again so eager, recondite with discovery. All my senses melded into sight. The pine chill, and woodland breeze, the crackling branches, and lilting bird sounds traveled through my eyes. A pair of hands fumbled with the tie on the canvases. They were my own hands operating in a vacuum devoid of touch and response. I could see them on the folded corners, the sound of the tethers unknotting. Saw around me a wavering heat, and everything external was mute.

Illumined now in the foreground of the glow, lay the lost paintings of Aìsling.

Wherein she showed so much of female rites, concealments, and uncomplicated objects lone in their beauty. She showed an unending love for Dallin. A colorful attenuation of an excruciating New Hampshire childhood. Trestle fields and well brooks. Alcoholic neglect. A love affair with insects. Jazz and bluegrass soundtracks to nights alone. She showed the images of girlhood wishing to the stars. A conversation with a turtle about what it must be like to live underwater. Nor'easter ice-coats, father slipping in a frozen dooryard. Hip broke. Blood spurts and blackouts. Solitudinous train travel through eastern Canada. At an island retreat, "ridiculous people who paint themselves painting." Gourmet cigarettes put out on white windowsills and Dallin's orange peels. Spiritual ascendency. Immanence, infinity. Deep, benevolent qualities: primates, skunk-companion, and feline. Play and comfort are principled, divine. Her mother's funeral,

Dallin a pillowy, abstract figure situated at her side. Her tears, little violet pedals, floating down from her cheeks through the air. The canvases progressed rapidly through age. There were many within the house on Coastal Road. One of the lighthouse in a rain storm, a blinking Hadean beacon. She showed the tone of life struggle and alter. Dreamed secrets locked within cubes of glowing light, textured with abstract talismans. A violin stretching from the player's hand over the ground fanning into paths of fate toned by variations of warmth, warnings, and smoke. A life filled with curious signs and messengers. I could sense in the last paintings what I had before in the house. Torn roots, violent change. The faces of the dead within snow-covered trees; black falcons. She showed a wooden shack, and a furious charcoal sketch almost obliterating the shape of a black typewriter. She tangled a candle's flame to frame the entire canvas with fire. In another, a sleeping head dreams a cloud, and in that cloud a troop of militarists march up a long road, a brutal man at the head, clouds of dust behind him. And spread in the dimensional sky above, in the red of blood, of wine, shouts one word: "*Pime.*"

Sprawled amongst the paintings scattered on the hillside, an immense affection arose for her at once. All the qualities of the paintings started to infuse into everything I knew. If Dallin was inside me—occasionally manifested in a realm that was mine, or within something I accessed too—if that is how I was related to Dallin on the interior, then I now felt immersed in Aìsling, as if she were everything external to me, everything outside my becoming interior, which included the exteriority of my body itself.

But this stir disgusted me, hot in the tumult, kneeling in the burgeoning light, betrayed. A burst shot up from my gut and I shouted it aloud, "*betrayed!*" By all I had devoted. By everything demanded in me by Dallin, I had been consumed, turned around, so deviated from any intention or resolution, sprawled there in the forest, immense with sorrow, with idiocy and rage, with a look of return to a stack of wood and canvas announcing so plainly, and quite shamefully, that I was owed something. "What am I doing out here?" Nothing. Just sat there in dirt, breathing. The atmosphere started to choke me. "Did he just want someone else to know what he had gone through, to find what he had lost? To discover how he died? . . . How Aìsling died?" But nothing in the paintings or the poems could help me know that. "Give me the knowledge of an ending at least," I thought, "so that for anything this can end as a dream."

A crash. And then another.

The trees around me were picked up in an uneasy ballet, the tips of lean branches blowing to the ground. The paintings were at my feet as I stood staring into a hazy gradient of descending colors. The abrupt noises re-awoke my senses. Skin, soaked in sweat; the stink of my death-suit. Big plumes of air rushed over my face, and for the first time since I had arrived there, in flight from the house, so eager in search of fact, in the guileless affirmation of fate, in deduction from the reality of death the possibility for life, I hadn't really considered the area surrounding me. That is, until the loud cracks grew nearer and began coming down from above.

The light was now much brighter, and my face grew hot. Air was being sucked away from my mouth and from behind my back. I sought for an area where it was continuous enough to breathe. The flaring light brought a larger area into sight, as though it were high day. I came around the edge of a thick grouping of trees which only provided entrance back into the body of the forest. Once around that corner where the tree line thinned, I was snared at, then singed, by an orange dragon of flame. A storming fire blared through the trees. Tall trunks were bursting in half, burning canopies of spruce toppling down to earth. I turned away, crouched before it in a terrible, naked light whose cause was complete obliteration.

I'd fallen, turned, then ran in the other direction. There was fire at the other end now, too. Big, singular thuds hit the dirt, shaking the entire ridge. Metal shells shone between fire and moon, glimmered through the pine stocks before falling and exploding into flame. Plane engines roared overhead, sounding through the fierceness of the burning sky. I was coughing relentlessly, and no matter how hard I could not inhale one single breath. The earth whirred and spun in circles. "What am I," "where is she," "who fire," "what plane," my head was sent toward the dirt. Vision periscoped the earth, and periphery sank into shadow. As soon as I fell, the shadows appeared. My heart yearned for the flailing of one of my arms, for the introduction of a coughing crawl on hands and knees in the direction of the jeep. It was over, I thought. A tightness in my chest restricted inwards until I was convinced in my ailing moment that any movement would snap me apart into pieces.

I faded away into the brown bed of dust.

When the earth is inaudible there seems to be at least a chance for peace. The giants crank the scum-shit jack clockwise with bulging, masturbatory forearms, until the pools in basement F backflow and the water settles. The flood, it lessens. Then there is a silent thanksgiving in the unconscious. No music, no guests, no orchestra left. They suffered a severe deportation order, effective immediately, but their instruments and folding chairs made interesting enough clacks and bangs and clouds of auricular noises by themselves. But no noise without an ear; the clown still don't worry when it sleeps—like I said, no guests there, which is why I was surprised by what happened next.

Up from the basement cellar and the gymnasium the shape of a silver hand arose, tempting me with all that I could ever desire. A man, "where from?" I meant to ask, but couldn't speak. "From the Horn of Plenty," he answered anyway. I was floating back to the surface, all sealed up for the journey. My lips were dried, closed. But he raised a finger to them, full of the scents of seeds and all the fruits, leaves, stocks, grains, flowers, vines, and trees that grew in the deep of where he had come from. His skin seamless, silver, and blue. Black on the folds, edges, and tucks. He got my spit flowing through the straw. (But my body still a bag of dead.) The spring trickled underneath but the brook, when looked at from above—the straw grass, lilies, leaves, bogs, and water—was still all frozen stiff. I was laying on the ground somewhere, I had a faint vision of it, one of mute brilliance, of myself away from myself, ha, *immajuhn dat*, laying on the ground, all over it, in one place, skin rubbery and tight from the cold or the heat. My red little muscles twitched occasionally, independent of bone and each other. Held my breath forever. I saw, to the side of me, quiet, glowing trees between the tent posts of the Cornucopian man's legs, where I reached up between them, rhythmically push-fisting and pull-gripping. The tighter I choked his joint the more it parted his lips in a wry smile. Within his mouth, now opened wide, a chrome butterfly spread its wings to each side, his tongue glistened and pulsed inside. When he leaned down towards my face sweating in the cold he let it drop out, and licked a wet strip across my closed lips. Now they were open, too.

The light liquids were mixing. He began to stroke me between the legs with a gentle hand. No bed talk about lovely destruction. The pressure pitch was infecting the inaudible seal I was sewn into, and, sure enough, it sounded like a leak. Out my mouth went little squeaks; the world seeping back in, slowly.

Falcons wove black nets of solitude. I fell upon those nets. There were pits of expired ember and ash whose bottoms emptied out in some opposite hole in space. I turned upon that listless vacuum.

At the crest of this precipice I felt bloodwater churning and the blue boy beating and the legless prayer whinnying and *woe* I murmured *woe* be me and *woe* my brain *woe* my charcoal throat *woe* to my scrotum I know I said without a sound coming up from inside *woe* to the low point *woe* to the eyes with two black diamonds blocking the light *woe* to thee *woe* but there are things that demand my attention *woe* and I know that sometime soon God will dawn but woe I said to *that* day.

I sang back my woes (and sorry I was), but I continued my toss down the spiraling arm. "Forget you, ghostly loves." "Forget you Mr. Mind, and Mrs. Divine. Betrayers, mine. . . ."

Soon, I was able to feel my thumbs, wriggle 'em, then whole hands, then limbs. My core was warming, heat flowing and pouring out on the surface. My hand still jerking, he jerked me back. Soon, kaplow. I began coughing in a fit but I laid back down. He said he realized that I was growing sick and asked me what it was. I said I didn't know. His hand quickened as he jerked at my stiff base, my breath increased. The silvery mouth smiled then mentioned something about the idiocy of laying out there in the woods like that. The murky bastard began to make fun of me, told me not to hope for so much, that my love affair with the poet's wife was tawdry and ridiculous. "Ridiculous!" I wanted to say, but couldn't yell, still barely able to speak. But it was starting to come back. He said I was childish for getting caught out there bare-assed and almost becoming burned to death. He chuckled, then rubbed the side of my face. With my little energy I swatted him away, he jerked faster. He said "stupid" for feigning sleep out there from my excited breathing of smoke. Stupid stupid stupid. My stupid singed throat. Stupid sore eyes. My stupid hard cock. Stupid dirt lullaby. Instant night and stupid tears for stupid sights. My sick, sick desperation. "Pump hurt cool soothe me," my stupid copious night man, "bring me back with your horn of stems and flower acids, bate me with your intangible hand, and impregnable mouth." "Would you like to know what happened to your poet and his precious wife?" he asked. I tried to sit up but he shoved me back down, concerned, still pleasure breasted and groin pummeled. I couldn't think. "How could he . . . ?" "But there's no . . .," my jaw tightened and my eyes turned inside as I pumped out a saucer of pearly milk all over his gripped hand.

My sight dimmed in and out through the crack of relaxed lids, he waited. "You're done," he said. The machinery of my breath then started. Lips parted, I exhaled. A tuft of gray smoke tangled up from my mouth, and I kept on blowing it out. It continued winding upwards until the breath was finished and all my damage was repaired.

This smoke plumed in the air above us. Earth sounds rushed back upon me in an onslaught. Weight; conscious; breathing again. I was exhausted. Raising my head to look for him, I squinted through the trees, where I saw a body further up. The night man was running away from me! A striding form of blue curves and silver outlines was losing its distinction to the pre-dawn light, his one glazed hand still shining, I watched as it bobbed away through the dark silhouettes of trees. In his naked flight across the grass in the direction of a far off street, which was even further up out of the woods, he turned and looked back at me. Yes, I remember it clearly now. Because when he turned back his face deconstructed into a thousand fires, that, when put together in a bon, in the naïvely compromised "livid flame," had no chance of ever resembling a person.

THREE

HIGH PITCHED NOTES DOVE FAINTLY in song upon me, once out of the woods, moving on worn tracts of grass through a block of buildings. There, a small girl sat, responsible for the inveigling song. Her heels hit along the bottom of an iron grate, sending out idiophonic clangs as waves toll from an old bell, from a linen dress of blue flowers.

The sun shone in the sky above as she sat on the first floor of the escape, and, walking up to her, I stopped, at the butt of the last hanging ladder rung. The sound of the iron being struck faded and the enormous vibrating apparatus that ascended up the side of the tan bricks ceased to shake. But, in that declining vibration, she proclaimed to know me. "How do you know me? If you do, I apologize, because I do not know you, dear." "I recognized you when you ran out to the corner over there. Why were you in the woods? You're all dirty," she said, resting her chin on a middle bar of the escape curling with black paint. "You are such a mess, silly, you look so tired. If I didn't know who you were I'd think you were scary, but you're not." A vague quality of remembrance concealed itself in her face, demeanor, and tone, but of what I didn't know. Someone I had known, or even touched? A woman that I might have loved, if I hadn't. . . .

In the absence of recollection, she carried on. "Where were you coming from just now?" "Fire," I stepped closer, "I just came from a fire." "Oh! Are you okay? Is that why you look so tired?" "I don't know. I'm fine." "You don't know?" "Yeah, what do you mean, I look tired?" "Like you haven't slept in a long time." "What are you doing sitting up there? Do you live here?" "I like to wait up here. Are you sick?" "Yes. What is it you wait for, exactly?" She laughed melodiously. I'd gotten used to it already in the short time standing there. An acute shadow formed narrowly along the wall opposite the sun. I was contemplating moving over to it, to take advantage in the shade, but before I could do so she shot up and straightened her flowery dress. "I'm coming down now," she said, "just wait for me, please."

Forest shadows recast faint, barely recoverable dream figures . . . a blue man, standing over me in a fiery haze, which then posed the question if those shadows in the forest were the same from the house on Old Coastal Road, had they come from the house after I fled? Were they following me? Returned, quickly, to revel in the familiarity of the girl, whose presence seemed to settle a tension within. *What the hell happened in that house, why were Aìsling's paintings in the wall, had they ever been seen, how had that fire come straight from the sky, what was that blue man who came out of night?* These questions swirled inside when she appeared from the side door saying, "can I walk with you?" She wanted to go to the shore, and asked me to take her.

We began to walk, I was trying to figure out what secret comfort she kept in walking with me, an unknown man. She sang "roses are red," while dragging her outspread hands low across the violet beds. When she looked over I noticed that, when standing with me, the sun never hit her face. More focus found her presence only more evasive. And I knew I was supposed to be looking for something which I had originally set out for, but it too evaded me. A distance had been formed by the shock of all that had happened, and it kept me from experiencing anything directly, leaving me to continue on unknowingly with the girl.

As we passed the north edge of the town, she told me the story of a drug blasted aunt who watched after her when her father slipped one winter, landing him briefly in the hospital. The woman would take her on long pilgrimages to crack-stale apartments in tenements along gross, industrial rivers. She was left there with moaning strangers while her aunt disappeared into one of the many rooms, returning tired, sometimes with her hair tossed or her lip split, throwing her into a cold car, where the aunt would get into the driver's seat with a metal pile of keys in hand and fall asleep. Sometimes they slept in the car all night. And in the summers, instead of the rusticated drug dens, she was brought to this coast, and was left alone on the boardwalk which we strolled.

To one side the gray waves of the Atlantic leapt and crashed white caps into rolling foam, and to the other side was the town, out of season, boarded up, and for the most part abandoned. The cold air bit, but the sea seemed to imbrue her, saying, "if you look, it's always changing, but I always say 'there's the ocean, let's go to the ocean,' thinking it's always the same, though it never is," the sea's roar all but eviscerated the rest of her observations. Mute to me, she skipped on the stones of the seawall, continuing on. I smiled, as though I understood. Her eyes were bunched by a big smile underneath her cheeks, and a spectacular twinkle gleamed there. Her mouth was red and wrapped with laughter, though something was strange, I knew that face, the sparkling eye, her wistful speech, and black, flowing hair. ". . . *Had I?*"

Traveled inland away from the coast, crossing an overpass where bits of trash were blown by weak cyclones. The trees caught the same breezy gusts. I poised to indulge, but it passed. She was leading me somewhere, and although I was the elder and the heavier, I don't know if I could've stopped her even if I had demanded it, for she led me not only by hand but by a yearning she'd sensed in me, by the handle of that fear whose multiple avenues intersected and crashed in me at all times. Well aware of this (and my weakened health), that little hold increased, leading past condemned dwellings and ruined cinder walls out to a clearing where the surrounding woods irregularly enclosed a vast, empty lot. The trees formed a wall so deep it appeared depthless, such like placid water. I hadn't any idea how big those trees were, how deep that forest in front of me was, until I was before it. The idea of immersing back within the woods, given my last tryst with death, was cringing, but to much relief this was not our destination.

"It's this way," she said, looking over her shoulder. A ways out a large wall ascended from the dirt made of rubber tires stacked in voluminous rows and precariously large piles. Circling along the wall, she found an entrance, a winding dirt path which I traveled to the end, and on the other side the girl's silhouette was framed in the exit, a petite body towering in a window of blue, pillared aside by masts of black columns. I came up next to her coughing, where, over the wall, before the forest line, my gaze extended out on a deep pit scattered with hundreds of decommissioned, disregarded, and utterly destroyed yellow buses.

It was hard to believe we'd reached our destination. "Isn't it beautiful?" she asked. I was thinking about Aìsling and that word, *Pime*. "What does that mean, that word? Pime pime Pime pime. . . ." "Hey! do you like it?" Sun in my eyes, I told her no. She turned, perturbed. ". . . Why? Because its dirty? How come you don't like filth?" "What? It's because I don't have any idea where I am, nor, I mean look at this, what are we doing out here? Who are you? You know what, never mind. I've got to get out of here—" "I think because it's the opposite of control, and you love control, don't you? You love it so much that you appear as if it didn't matter to you at all," that mouth uttered, from a face nearly translucent, yet depthless as the daytime distortion of the tree line. She ran ahead and climbed down, disappearing into the monuments of jagged metal and twisted axles, long glimmering roofs, smashed windows, and bare steel frames. Among the wrecked fleet below she had already passed from sight. Then, a faint "come on . . ." snuck quietly over the mound descending from the bank.

Dusty air stung in the disorientation of the high sun. A safe direction emerged but I navigated my way poorly, wracked by bouts of debilitating nausea. Laughter echoed through the rusted, rigid obstructions that restricted most movement. Thinking only for a moment of losing her in that horrid place, my pace quickened, and in that searching a strange euphoria was found, as though she hid from me on purpose. I was overcome with joy that I was playfully chasing my own daughter, one I'd never had, throughout a world of wrecked buses, hidden niches, and intriguing, unpredictable paths.

Around the side of one of the buses I eventually found her, propped up on the edge of a large metal hood, draping her legs over the front. Shoe heels striking the tall engine grill shot metallic shocks off the black slats as the mallets of her feet banged upon the bus. I approached, breathing heavily, prepared to scold the disappearing act. "Do you know why I'm sitting on this bus?" she asked abruptly. "I don't—," she hummed again, roses and blue violets, but it sounded wrong, something was pulling it downward. Again, she asked the question. "I told you, I don't know." I asked why she'd made me follow her down there, but she just repeated the same simple question. "What do you want me to say! All the buses are the same." "This one I am sitting on," smacking her palms flat on the hood, "its special." "Well how would, I mean, how am I suppose to. . . ." "A23D8E87," she said factually. "Excuse me?" "A23D8E87." ". . . It's cold, I've never been here this time of year." "So you've been here before?" Hands now folded, she nodded yes. To the side of the bus, where the doors were folded closed, underneath the first passenger window, I found the number A23D8E87.

Back around to the front, I asked her to stop playing games and told her I was leaving. After a durative, windy pause, she murmured, "I was raped in this bus." This gentle effusion incinerated the air between us; her speech and my broad, turned back. A lump tightened in my throat, and I returned, climbing up to sit next to her. ". . . *What?*" I asked her, "when?" She was looking down at her hands, picking away at something. "*Hey, when?*" I took her hand, covering it with mine. "It's okay, you can tell me." She looked up with tears shaking both eyes, then faced her head back down and shook it continually, no. "You know, it's alright . . ." "*You don't remember, do you?*" "Remember what?" ". . . that it was you. *You raped me here.*"

I forced an immediate objection, but objected nothing. A strong vacuum of silence tore through my weak stomach, sore lungs, my heart, all my gears, my blood, everything. I couldn't recall a thing. Bereavement collided with a spinning, nauseous refutation. "I didn't," and muttered more suspicious defenses, but I knew before I knew: her angelic, light smile, and hurt but loving gaze, the delicate way tears fell from her face. Then, on the cold hood, listening to her exhaled breaths, *a film of white light washed over my eyes*, and I saw her, laid there on the hood of that same bus, dress fanned out, a shadow draped between her legs. A large hand gripped across her throat; . . . yet she lay still, deathly complacent. At the back of her head the hand twists full of black hair, dirty pants bunch at the feet, and he begins to rock into her thighs. *Another flash*. Palms, fingers smudge little wipes across the windshield, her face is turned away. Now he kneels behind her, knees scrape and tear, blood gurgles in its opened holes. She turns over and looks back, suddenly, she is older, face is longer, deeper, her eyes widely vibrant and bold, and she smiles, . . . her petite frame continues to shake, violently possessed from behind, . . . her expression though, glows, coquettish and joyful, I recognize her, but as a woman, having kissed the mirage of her lips, slept in the softened nape of her long neck, we loved, we were night, once. My call to her is returned by a coarse cry of love to terror, and instantly the beautiful mystery flows back into a bloody rape child, turned back again, horrified and naked on the glass, slapping of pink, fuck-warmed flesh syncopating the last deep, hurtful howls of two previously separated bodies conversing in the trade of rape, kindle this vision as I struggle to break free from, snap! *Another flash.* His large hand crashes through a crack along the windshield, glass ripping up his arm, which, told by his face, overtakes the pleasure of his crotch, finally killing the determined rhythm. Then, the screaming begins again.

Her hair came down and choked me. Her hair was the hair of all. All the hands that rubbed me away were too the hands of one. The anonymous. The apparition. Her back the gleaming back of all. Her breasts of all breasts. Tears of all tears. Her face the Crying Face. Her warmth, my warmth. And her youth, my youth.

When I broke from the sudden violence of the vision my hand was completely covered in blood. I'd fallen from the front of the bus to the ground, where I crawled around confused in crippling agony.

Eventually I righted myself, stood in pain, and looked around on top of the bus and all around the pit, but she was gone. I was there alone. The insides of my pants were soaked, the waft of rough sex and angelic abuse rose from my waist, a mixture of come I later assumed, but it was unclear whose it was. *Why was she a woman, when was she child, when was she old, had I known her, when had I fallen, where did she go?*

On my way out of the dusty heap I reached the dirt embankments and walked on through the disparate, open fields. It was clear I needed to abandon this search for good and find my way back home. Though I still heard Dallin, sifted through libraries and condemned buildings, fell in burning forests and treacherous pits, even though I had read the poet's familiar and gracious words and was fortunate enough to have seen the wonderful forgotten images of Aìsling, I had been lead so far away, my sickness was worsening, waist was blue with bruises, my conscience reflected in a thousand broken chards an image of incomprehensible confusion and cruelty. My previous excitement which had turned to raging guilt had now given way to resignation, my arm at my side wrapped in the strips of a sweater swelling with blood.

It was dark and I was back in my apartment. Aìsling's fate needled me at every point, and Dallin's long absences were worrisome. I sat against a wall in the living room, the soles of my slippers stuck against the wooden floor, slipping an inch more with each cough. My head a flaming metronome, forth, with scorn for randomness, appearance, non-connectivity; and back again into the wall, *bang!*, for the affirmation of intent, the stinging hint that causality existed before its useless activation by a blubbering, poetic machine.

Kept time with Time. Stared blankly with watery eyes into a city that lost its night. Took my cocktail glass engraved with hopeful gray stars and my stinking bottle of Jameson from the floor, and, over at the window, rested my forearms on the white sill, pouring from the bottle an amber drop. The light invaded me, broke my blackness into pockets for surpassing, transgressing. The light came in through the green glass, spiking through the whiskey kaleidoscope into an array of designs that made slaves of the eyes. In an exhausted effort to make myself cry, my hands were wrapped upon my face, and still smelled like the vagina of an unknowable age. Looking closely, dirt was still tightly caked under my fingernails. I put the tips into my mouth, resting them lightly on the bottom row of teeth. My mouth was shaking; tongue (a drunken boat in a shallow salivary sea) touched the salty tops as I opened my teeth, weakly, in an attempt to bite out the dirt. The taste was foul and I withdrew, staring off into the landscape of buildings; drool strung between my hand and lip sank itself down into my lap. I seeped out one weep that cracked into a smile that ached. Another cannon of whiskey set ablaze my cage of organs. Soothed my scum tunnel. I fell to my ass and left the bottle on the window, floating back into the moment of lightness falling weightless ageless freedom. . . .

My head went back hitting the wood floor with a thud, eyes peeled wide inside blue lids. I was laying in a bed of violets. . . . Sprawled out on the planks, across my entire floor *a patch of wild violets*! Smile bent wide, a film of joy came over my eyes.

I wait for the cream horse of dawn and the obsidian horse of dusk to collide on the horizon, to reveal what they must.

Everything between was still my dream. Old Massachusetts. Worms devouring a thin dog at the end of a street in Budapest. Friends hung in midnight's trees. Uneven fields in France where grass and poppies grow over previously plowed tank treads. Dormitory sluts in the District of Columbia forgetting themselves at the conquered peaks of their anthill orgasms. My drunken smirk was planting cancer in the roofs of all their pink garages. I wondered why these were ideas or truths. Why hadn't I didn't know. Couldn't be bothered, felt like the skin of a cunt pushed through, broke wide open, a breath of fresh air taken, and let out to the world. Violets perfumed my vision and festooned the feet of my letters. Memories of Yeats cased themselves together in full sentences, then ran free in Irish meadows. From my chest a river churned forth, and from its waters my arms raised up, the one scarred, diced with incisions made by shattering glass, writhing; and it was there, God damn it, I began to think.

"That these flowers are for a funeral, that this is my grave."

That the future is a grave. That appearance is a grave, "... and I, only a grave of appearance?" And that talk show hosts have graves. Grandfather (who played guitar and built ships in bottles, who drank and abandoned his family) has a grave. The goalie from my youth league hockey team has a grave (hanging by an orange extension cord from his garage door track). That old Henry, Kenneth, Marguerite, and Alain, John, George, and Charles, Marianne, e.e., W.G., Robert, Thomas, and Franz. Neil, Jacks, the two Bens: tits&ass (T&A) and gin&tonic (G&T), old friends from the river. Jean, Ezra, Dylan, Sylvia, Bill, Alan, and William, Bueneventura, Giambattista, Gregory, Augustus, Vlad, and Rimsy. Old Herbert, Wallace, William, and Byron, who too extolled the Dying Gaul ... All I have forgotten is a grave. The moment before this has a grave. That moment before this one, and so on.... "So where did all these flowers come from? ... IS THIS MY GRAVE? *Have you come to hear the speech?* Because I promise, there won't be one."

My laughter felt the tips of the petals my fingers could not. There is nothing like the mixed smell of vagina, whiskey, and flowers; my hands for once were a lovely place to be! The bottle was still sucking in the light from the night-tried city. The universe did the same through me. My elation calmed around the same time a clock tolled in the distance unsure of the time and my mouth dried up around the edges and in the back at my throat, where, on my back, I laid facing upward, feet turned outward, propped up on bare elbows. And there, in the far corner, near the wall of windows at the front of the room, a flower, a dark, red flower,

. . . . o n e s i n g l e r o s e . . . .

was sticking out above the rest. It bent heavily over the many free and easy violets, so, naturally, I scorned it: ". . . why?" My brow sank deeply into lines, then my whole face filled with blood. No more frolicking countenance. I rose to my feet on the only patch of bare floor amidst the living room of flowers, those perfect flowers and this rose. This rose tore me away from my drunk Spring, from that elation of memory and form mixing in lightness, freely! (Ho ho, remember *that* proclamation?) It came into my consciousness as lightning cracks the dome, creating again the distance of darkness and light. I went over to the windowsill and re-soaked myself, then turned and stood there wavering, staring, breathing long and deep, bottom lip shining in liquor.

"A'fuck're you doing here," I asked the rose. Silence. Real silence; just the pitiful sound of the human remaining. "Why now!" I roared, then slow sobbing overtook the room.

The room lost its glow, only vague illuminations strayed faint and charmless across the space. The lights from outside came in through the bottle and back out in all directions, down onto my delicate steps toward the rose, where, carefully, my heel came down between each blue flower cup, . . . to toe, next heel, then toe, and so on across the Rubicon. Standing before it, fighting the urge to feel glad that I was taller than it, I looked down into its deep, red eye, then knelt next to the swirling, divine proportion. A ghostly hand gripped the back of my neck, urging me towards it, as though I were being punished. "For what," I asked grittily, pissed. "For giving up? Why should I be forced," I cried, "what am I being faced with?" Discarded by happiness, dethroned of lightness, the malevolent exception held me there, captive. "In cloudy eye, past haze, a mistakable patch of sweet flowers," and grief, slowly erupting upward. "I do not know; how (a sob a sob), *how can I not know. . . .*"

Reaching down, the rose petals between my thumb and forefinger were of the softest silk, kind, in a way consoling of the eternal loss they emblemized so well, surrounded, of course, by thorns on all sides. I laughed at the nature of its abstract power. The abstract power of nature laughed back, resolutely. "Why am I being laughed at, Dallin? Why do you meddle in this misery? Manifest great lengths to provoke me? I am trying to climb over the hill of myself! Or come down! Why destroy my plateau? Because it's built with spiritless dirt? Because I am ...Shivering inside? Tortured by a voice? Why couldn't I have just continued on, nonsensical to life? Wrap myself comfortably in forgetting? The fade of memory's lace? . . . oh, I know it. I know! Humans hate their science! Looks to other truths, then away from those truths, too! But that is not what I asked you, you who escapes me. Are you, as you said, in *the air between the birds?* Are you within the *why why why?* Now I am too, and I want to die. Are you lost in mighty fucking evergreens that scrape the sky, the shit-of-names, Rose, Death's processes? The little girl said the ocean is always changing, that it makes its limits an integral part of its Whole." (We mock ourselves through the ocean.) "Right. And the sky mocks us with eternity."

(SHUT THE FUCK UP WITH THAT RUBBISH. THIS IS HOW YOU SPEAK TO YOURSELF, IN TEXTBOOK MONOLOGUES, BEAT-BIBLE, BATH-HOUSE TRASH?) "WHAT SHIT SEPARATIONS I'VE MADE OF LIFE!" (YES! BUT WHAT'S THIS 'I' NOW? LET'S GET DOWN TO IT, HANG FROM THAT LOOSE THREAD!) "I'M IN THE NARROWS, AND I, . . . I, CRANIAL, FRAYING, MIND, JUST FALL'N TO PIECES. EVER HAVE I BEEN ANYTHING BUT IN PIECES?" "OH, WHAT HAS *HAPPENED. . . .*"

(YOU, WRECKED CONSTRUCTION! EFFUSED, SICK FURY! COME UPON THE PRESENT, TO RETURN YOU MUST TRAVEL SO FAR AWAY . . . AND YOU'RE ALMOST THERE, YOU'VE GONE SO FAR, RAVEL DOWN, FRIEND! DEPART! DANCE! BOTTOM-DANCE, DOWN! ALONG THE TETHER AND ON OUT! ACROSS A THOUSAND GRAINS! A MILLION MINDS! BETTER TIMES! THOSE WHO NEVER DIED FOR YOU! AND THOSE FEW YOU'VE YET TO DISAPPOINT! RECEIVE THEIR DISAPPOINTMENT! THEIR INDIGNATION! LOVE IT, LOVE THEM, LOVE GOD, LOVE NEVER, LET YOUR HEART & FACE SLIDE OUT YOUR STRONGEST POINT—YOUR COCK, YOUR OVARIES, YOUR SMILE, DISCOVERY, POVERTY, PRIVILEGE, CHANGE, YOUR ONE IDEAL, YOUR FOUGHT FOR DREAM, YOUR WORN OUT KNEES, YOUR RELIGIOUS FAMILY, YOUR 'ROCK,' YOUR PRIZED RATIONALITY—*LOOK AT IT*, YOUR CHILDHOOD IS NOT INSIDE IT, YOUR COMMUNICATION PROBLEM IS NOT INSIDE IT, YOUR SEPARATION . . . NOT INSIDE IT, THE HATE OF THE WORLD RE-

SIDES NOWHERE, SAVE IN YOU, NOT IN BODIES, NOT IN BUILDINGS, NOT EVEN IN THE HEART; SO EAT IT, ENGULF IT AND BECOME *(your name)*, OVERCOME *(your name)*, NOT UNDERSTANDING IS YOUR ONLY SHAME. LIVE AMONGST OBJECTS YOU KNOW APPEAR DIFFERENT BECAUSE THEY ARE ALL THE SAME. LIVE AMONGST PEOPLE. LIVE IN FORESTS FAR. LIVE WHERE YOU FEAR. BE WHAT YOU DREAD. APPROACH ALL YOU ARE WITH A HAMMER, CLAW, CRITICISM, AND CARESSES. OBTAIN HALLUCINOGENIC MINDGLASSES & GET TO FUCKING WORK. THEN RE-THINK THE FACES, RE-THINK THIS WORLD & ITS SPACES, ENGAGE THE BLESSED TEDIUM OF REPAIRING ALL THAT YOU'VE DESTROYED, FROM MEMORIES TO ENTIRE LIFETIMES, THE CHAIR YOU BROKE APART TO ASK IT WHAT IT WASN'T, THE RED DOOR YOU DENTED UNDER THE ASSUMPTION THAT IT WAS NOT RED, THAT IT COULD NOT BE RED, THAT NO THING POSSESSES ITS COLOR, THAT YOU POSSESS ITS COLOR, YOUR EYE IS A BRUSH, AND YOUR MIND DOES THAT,

YOUR MIND PAINTS EVERYTHING,

THIS IS ALL YOUR DREAM—THE WORLD GAINED THROUGH THE EARS, THE EYES, BLARING OR QUIET, TEARY OR DRIED, THE WORLD LOVED THROUGH KINDNESS AND MEASURED BY TIME, THE WORLD THAT BLOSSOMS FIELDS OF DOOM, THE LINE OF FUTURE & PAST THAT LOOMS, CIRCLING AS YOU GO IN CIRCLES, THIS WORLD YOU WONDER ABOUT, DEFECATE IN, THE ONE THAT MAKES YOU TIRED AND ENDLESSLY MAD, THE WORLD YOU DREAM INTO IS YOUR DREAM, KNOW THAT YOU PUT SADNESS ON THEIR FACES, BLOOD IN THEIR DICKS, HATE IN THEIR MINDS, HOPE IN THEIR HEARTS, CALLUSES ON THEIR HANDS, PRISONS IN THEIR LANDS, JUDGMENT'S VEIL UPON THEIR EYES, LOVE IN THEIR CHEAPEST CREVASSES, *YOU ARE RESPONSIBLE FOR EVERYTHING, YOU DO NOT HAVE AN OPPOSITE, THERE IS NO SUCH THING AS AN ENEMY,*

THERE IS NO SUCH THING AS OBSCURITY,

DISASSEMBLE! RECONSTRUCT! PROVE YOU'VE NO NATURE! PROVE YOU'VE NO PREFERENCE! NO DISPOSITION! GRAVITY! PROVE HISTORY WRONG! PROVE THE UNIVERSE RIGHT!

ENTER THE PAINTING! THERE IS NO PAINTING! YOU ARE IN THE PAINTING! YOU ARE THE PAINTING BECAUSE EVERYTHING IS THE PAINTING! PROVE YOU NO SELF, DISSOLVE PETTY CHILD DISSOLVE PETTY CHILD EVOLVE PETTY CHILD OUT OF A PETTY CHILD

. . . . .INTO THE WORLD!

FUCK THIS, FUCK YOU, FUCK THE IDEA OF YOU!
(NO THIS NO YOU NO TO THE IDEA OF YOU)

WHAT ARE YOU SO AFRAID OF?
THE GODS ARE GETTING TIRED OF THIS.
THE UNIVERSE IS GETTING TIRED OF THIS.
"I" AM GETTING TIRED OF THIS.
THIS IS GETTING REAL *TIRED* OF THIS.

"Oh my, I don't mean to startle you, a discussion amongst friends mustn't be so grandiose, . . . IT'S JUST THAT THE PARENTHESES NEVER CLOSED. What the fuck are we to do now? We can't just have everybody's parentheses open and the secrets told, . . . *where is everybody?*, pouring the junk of ourselves upon the world, . . . *where are all the people?* Berto? If you can hear me, have Jacob's parentheses closed? Has it yet been revealed, the criteria of our responsibility? Harmony can't be right. I think that I am beginning to understand, . . . *where are you all?*, I am ready now. I said I didn't mean to startle you and I am sorry. Wait, who am I talking to. No, I am not sorry. Who is talking. What—"

The rose remained between my fingers. Its weight was so light, so grave, so infinite and so implicating that I just couldn't—, I moved my hand down the flower's stem, gripped its green base, and yanked upwards as hard as I could. The pain of the moment the pain of me the pain of the flower shot through my arm, letting go. I turned over my hand, a line had formed across my palm; perfect red bubbles swirling with blood. I choked it back. My face inverted, insides burned. Then, the blood droplets broke, and bled into intersecting lines. I roared again through clenched calcium; my gritted teeth locked shut with rage. Reaching back down to where the flower met the floor I ripped up the tall rose, crumbling it in my wounded palm. I tossed the crushed flower across the room, spraying a dotted line of blood down the wall and over all the violets that stood before me. Red drips on blue petals, I trampled through the flowers into the bedroom, slamming the door behind me.

Strange out here lately. Nuns with microphones pinned under their habits, deadweight standing on old boards outside a motel room door, waitresses and aid workers that were spooked by their obvious contact with the sinister.

We've stayed ahead of all of it, somehow, but it is a matter of time before they come, and they will. It is the will of this man, this soldier who pursues us by bounty. His name is Pime Malius. He is the agent who has been given the task to murder Aisling and to murder me, along with many more whom we don't know.

This is what we are escaping, what caused us to flee our home. This brutal sentinel broke in one night, attempting to take us alive. But we anticipated it, and made it out just in time. But I can't view that as any type of success, with no refuge left in the country and traveling in the dead of winter, on foot, most other modes of travel cut, I regret to admit we are running out of options.

Lt. Malius' reputation certainly precedes him. His weight and size are twice that of another man. Towering, and forceful, his gruesome determination functions at the behest of the State, he is their chief bounty hunter and political assassin, a full time job in the recent conflicts. He is of military discipline, psychotic, and powerful, has been to battle on every major continent, and thrived in military fields of slaughter, in Yancheng, the unnamed provinces of Islamabad, the Ports of Chester, Tarabulus, and most recently at home, the Chesapeake Bay massacre. He fought all over, and when the war began here, Pime was offered to lead a special intelligence unit, whose jurisdiction is basically unknown. He began making military arrests at the colleges. In time, he went from students to professors, and I was one of the first targets, using the controversy of my wife and I as examples of the transition from protestors to widespread threats to national will and security, moving past Aisling and I to include a wider array of rebels, militia leaders, and 'terrorists,' to use the elusive parlance. People have exaggerated to me his lust to see his victims die personally, saying he grows nearly extra human when imbued by death.

So, he has declared his intention to kill us, for my role at the University, and the books I wrote, for Aisling's recent influential works, and I suppose in general the trouble we are viewed as having contributed to, which the regimes of governance have decried as not just pitiable, but beyond all justification.

As for our situation, people are being helped through some warehouse building on the water in the next city and from there they are being moved out of the country. I have been assured that this is safe, but I am not foolish. Ash and I finished packing, and tonight we will leave, to where I don't know. What I fear is, once we start running again, allow ourselves to be chased, we are again exposed to the possibility of death (as if there were a time we never were) but I sense, somehow, that this is the last stretch, and we have no choice but to be ready, and be willing to greet whatever does come. Perhaps Aìsling and I will arrive at something that, in the realm of life's fantasy, will supersede the vileness which is upon us.

I loved them both, you see, becoming this event, that event, because of it, hung up on each aspect of the mystery of their disappearance. Did you think I was without fault? I loved Dallin, for his poetic entry into life, and Aìsling for acrylic nightmares, for my reminiscence of a long past feminine temperament, and the rest of it. Aside this love, though, I was flippant, innerved. Yes, frustration. Yes, denied intuition. Yes, relentless procurement of imaginary, possible, tangential, hopeful, and actual, serene considerations. Robbed of possessing even a notion outside of cruelty. . . . In anger, I tore at my jacket and twisted it in the air, silently demanding of it answers, ones I needed to know. When I threw it to the couch, I ran to the bathroom down the end of the hall, vomiting.

Dense fog dispenses the plain as though these clouds form and grow in a field, from the ground up. The moisture on the window-panes blocks the dawning sun from entering the cabin at all. My bones creek when I move. Wrapped in a blanket, I've been up for hours, watching Aisling sleep. We left camp yesterday and traveled until this morning. Began typing a while ago in order to stay warm while keeping watch, but only recently words such as DENSE FOG DISPENSES, and, BONES WINDOW DAWN have started to come out. One arm extended from the folds of my blanket punches A A A A A A A A A A A A A A A A A A A A A A A A A A A A A A A, da, da, da, da da, da da, da da, da da dada dada dada dada dada dada dada dadA DaDa DAda daDA daDA daDA daDA daDA daDA daDA daDA daDA DADA DADA DADA DADA DADA DADA DADA DADA DADA DADA DADA DADA DADA DADA DADA DADA DADA DADA DADA DADA DADA DADA DADA DADA DADA DADA DADA DADA DADA DADA DADA DADA DADA DADA DADA DADA DADA DADA DADA DADA

DADA DADA DADA DADA DADA DADA DADA DADA DADA
DADA DADA DADA DADA DADA DADA DADA DADA DADA
DADA DADA DADA DADA DADA DADA DADA DADA DADA
DADA DADA DADA DADA DADA DADA DADA DADA DADA
DADA DADA DADA DADA DADA DADA DADA DADA DADA
DADA DADA DADA DADA DADA DADA DADA DADA DADA
DADA DADA DADA DADA DADA DADA DADA DADA DADA
DADA DADA DADA DADA DADA DADA DADA DADA DADA
DADA DADA DADA DADA DADA DADA DADA DADA DADA
DADA DADA DADA DADA DADA DADA DADA DADA DADA
DADA DADA DADA DADA DADA DADA DADA DADA DADA
DADA DADA DADA DADA DADA DADA DADA DADA DADA
DADA DADA DADA DADA DADA DADA DADA DADA DADA
DADA DADA DADA DADA DADA DADA DADA DADA DADA
DADA DADA DADA DADA DADA DADA DADA DADA DADA
DADA DADA DADA DADA DADA DADA DADA DADA DADA
DADA DADA DADA DADA DADA DADA DADA DADA DADA
DADA DADA DADA DADA DADA DADA DADA DADA DADA
DADA DADA DADA DADA DADA DADA DADA DADA DADA
DADA DADA DADA DADA DADA DADA DADA DADA DADA
DADA DADA DADA DADA DADA DADA DADA DADA DADA
DADA DADA DADA DADA DADA DADA DADA DADA DADA
DADA DADA DADA DADA DADA DADA DADA DADA DADA
DADA DADA DADA DADA DADA DADA DADA DADA DADA
DADA DADA DADA DADA DADA DADA DADA DADA DADA
DENSE, and FOG, finally. One finger punching
one frosted lever in the cold, until the fra
frah FROST shaves from inside the tiny metal
mechanisms and the locked-up keys begin to
warm and break free from continual tapping.

Lapping handfuls of water to my face brought no rejuvenation, repelled it even, but the mirror accepted me, took in all my face as I stood readying another rise in sickness. My deadpan eyes bulged and dried from the crying of all who have ever cried, then teemed with the duress of the absent tears of all the rest. A line had widened and widened still, from inner ear to inner ear, a deep blackened slit spreading across my face as a knife splits an oil-sick fish, blackness bled its drape of lace and my face stretched with a smile even longer. The entirety of this whole period (though I could not account for what had truly happened), could have been averted with a time worn wish, long past and unfulfilled, of folding my face into my eyes and laying to rest in the womb of my *yahdah yahdah yahdah*. You wouldn't had to have had the patience, the servility to my aimless voyaging and tiring inclinations toward self doubt. You should have shielded yourself from this. "Now look," the mirror stopped returning my image. "Good, now I'm pretty sure I've stopped reflecting anything solid."

It is true we are going to perish here, in this cabin, where Aisling lays now to sleep, and I nervously keep watch, still sitting over her, stroking her hair, weeping enough to cough on the cold with no relief, wiping the tears from my face before they freeze.

We will certainly perish here, yes. We have made a decision I never thought it possible to make. Her passage from this life will occur at dawn, tomorrow, and mine sometime later. This is all there is left to know.

Breath strict, and slow, eyes wide, tap done dripping on bowl of porcelain, silent. In the mirror, back through the cracked door out past the hall, my jacket hung from the couch. I stared at it toweling my hands. And I stood upright, yes upright, and stepped across the little turquoise tiles yes and traced back the ache still in my groin from the naked man of in-between hours and the rape I came rid of cough through that hall and stood at the foot of the couch staring at the gold tassel holding together a bowed fold of old pages. There it was, the poem from the bottom of the world, . . . picked up, and read.

THE RAPE AND MURDER OF AISLING

Panic's wretched gaze binds me, a promise has me chained.
By will of love, blindly, I'm fastened to a boundary maze
In wait of a feted torment. Brazen fields of gold wheat
Draw forth the fire from a young Sun, bring cold sky
Past its thin, sleepy nightmare towards the ascetic choir
That yawns out the dawn. Within morning mist,
A wooden shack divines my wife. Holy, preparatory,
She kneels within.

Each pull on my chain is a racket on the rail,
But the view ahead draws me quiet (she said to stay quiet).
A clamor quickens up the road's dregs, a pale globe, a rune
Of danger causes the ground birds to flutter back into Winter.
Up the road, Aìsling stands in the doorway of the shack,
Trailing a white dress, staring out across the field.
Further back, past sloped hills of wheat, my scribe
Hands record, and lowered eyes pray.

From my station on the hill it is clear who approaches,
Lieutenant Pime Malius and his soldiers drum up a cloud.
The distance between pomp and refuge shortens
And, silking through the dirt veil, she comes
Brushing her fingers low upon the violet cups
That blow from where she goes. Up, up along the iron road
Guns hang from an order of necks, the men
Stand around Pime, enclosed in a circle.
White raiment trails her frail feet
As Aìsling walks to the center and lifts her face
To the dark sentinel.

From over the hill, Pime grows in size, seething
In dust and brine. Teeth grit, bones click, heat raises up.
Head thrown, Malius grows, master of rank to Destroyer.
The wind on the fields and gray clouds
Keep from me the formality of Pime issuing a
Governmental decree, through which, though,
I hear Aìsling still humming so easily low,
Hymnal melodies! . . . It ends just then, when
Black arms bend and enfold her, rip her from the ground,
Garment lace dangling in the dust. When her shoulders drop
Her hair whips like an auburn flame, then her disciplined
Eyes close, serenely.

Chained, I bear my love taken. From her pure body,
Tethers are torn. Pime crashes down upon her, jumps at her neck,
And wild, rapes her. In the circle of guns he grows stronger
While Aìsling lays and does not struggle. Motionless and silent.
Grunts, yells, nothing. He hits her, slathers waste,
Drops his weight between her legs torn through
And worn to pounded bone. Her waist is fractured, split in two.
She keeps silent in all this, beneath her own slaughter.
Blood nearly drowns the Killer's victorious whispers
To Mars, but the whispers travel far, churning in my ear
Like violent gears. Locked to wood, I shake,
With every last twitch Aìsling makes.
His imbibing ritual closes with a long, waned growl,
The moon hides in high day, and an arisen Pime stands
Within her body, bleeding across the dirt.
. . . My love, is dead.

I sink to the ground, blinded, stinging.
I go out in parts and come back in,
Recovered from the bounds of mania, temporarily.
Ahead, where blood lay pooled and sprayed, Pime stands
In Aìsling's remains: hair, vestments, torn limbs,
Blooded gown, his dark circle glowing, though
Not by his doing. Aural light comes gathering in rings.
Frightened soldiers step back, leaving Pime alone
In the hum and the buzzing.

Zenith rouses dust! In blue break, light, and heat!
The moon back out to see
A wiser Pime tread the ground in horror,
Stagger, broke of balance, suddenly void of power.
The final denouement comes when he turns
And turns around himself, realizing
A dead angel has bested him, past murder.
His high size deflates, and Malius, warrior, beast,
Sentry of State, arrives past his apparent victory, to the end.
Shrunken down, revelation upon him, he turns
In the light of day, to the East, then rips his eye
Right from his face, cursing the passing doom of his fate,
Discarding it to the dirt. In the still, rolled eye, a shadow descends,
He falls from his feet, gripping a large stone.
His men watch as their leader drives his head
Upon the clutched boulder, over, and over,
Dying silently beneath the ceasing crunch of bones.
Pime fell next to the place where Aìsling lay,
& blood, charred this time, ran down around the stone altar,

Out from under the crippled legs draped from
A now headless vessel. Pime lay aside a body that was
At a past moment there, but which has now disappeared. . . .

The eye in the settled dust transmits
The result of that which Aìsling devised: a monster
Left motionless in suicide. And my final witness, I raise up,
Stripped of everything, to behold the flight and passage.
My wife, up from plight and ruined flesh, transforms
To infinite dawn, gleaming air, light through dusty fields
And far off trees, she bends, from in the beauty of Days,
And floats through the flux, a heaven of rest, forever
Free, and away.

From a bank on a massive, weeping river, the aquatic world cascaded down, raged and lulled, relieving both sickness and word. For once, there were no words. The watery refractions glistened and retracted. Slowly, I came to on the floor in a pile of written pages.

Certainly, I should have been disillusioned, deterred by discontinuous behavior, long distorted visions, drunkenness, and growing sickness, but what was there to disengage towards? What reality was there for me outside of this? I could take the late night rapes, I thought, the odd, illusory stints of impossible appeals to love. Love of any sort was not yet possible, because something enormous choked life from all over, and from all sides, from inside. There was never a sign of life, no bodies endowed by light, no one in the cars or parks or buildings, which were all around. Never a whim nor spoil, a chance encounter, an engagement until Dallin. I saw only various marks without quality on a line of negative integers all somewhere below one, and I was under the belief that this was correct, whole, complete, but then a voice came into my head such as I had never heard, suggesting value and wonder could survive suffering. And indeed it had in what was occurring within me.

A deeply known rhythm, an innate cohesion, his voice seemed to emanate (disregarding fixed affirmations of space) from the wellsprings of forever. He sang of lived life, even unbearably witnessing the death of his wife. What did I know about lived life, loving someone then watching them die? When I heard it I was attentive, and followed it when it came from the periphery and grabbed me, there, cowering at the center and dragged me to the outside. Or, oppositely, I was out there wavering at the lonely edge, and his voice came and evinced me of a center to life, that I could persevere, proceed from an origin, bare myself, *partake*. He woke me from some strange sleep and was forcing me to acknowledge it. He graced me with the beauty of his language, and brought to my eyes the colors not of a beautiful woman but the Woman of Beauty herself, who proved to me with astounding truth that she had been, that she was, that she will forever be. To this I wept. That horrific, beautiful poem, all his old pages, and all her paintings bred a point of reference in me; indications of involvement, becoming entwined. The indeterminate isolation which preceded the search had been connected to, linked to something I could refer to and hold.

So much broke through and fluttered. I began to flutter! To dream. Not to dwell, or to torturously envision, or to construct in order to destroy, but *to dream.* I would've been unbelieving of my disbelief, but I peered all the way back to the terrain of an earlier point of view, far back into my experience, like looking into the narrowing cone of younger and simpler light conflating back into the Bang, I envisaged it smoking in its complete disaster. I saw everything as a tall onerous house made all of one material, such as coral, breathing poison into itself, becoming calcareous and ornate, making the poison part of its walls and frame, an entire structure built up from clouds of psychotic gases. Teaming with the blackness of every disease, it sat, breathing on the edge of a cliff, appearing as sanctuary before the folly that the ledge impressed upon the wayfarer. A mirage of safe haven in the desert night. But, once past it, further down this plane, now with light and some tools to be able to see, it looked like death itself, built organically from fear and misery and, from where I was in the big chasm, the shift, the toppling and the transformation, the unrealized terms and the dangling bait of hope, where I was with delusions and voices deep in the breast of an empty world, I could see it coming apart, could feel the tremors rumbling across the flat terrain of desert where I stood just far enough past it to breathe, to begin to rejoice, to feel as though all was coming to a head, as if indications of life were just around the corner.

You see, I was that wayfarer turning away from himself, caught between the danger of the edge and the horror of the domicile. So, not wanting to choose a structure where within death would certainly consume me, nor the definite end that the edge of the plane suggested, I moved further along, carefully and defensively astray, until I'd gone far enough away to see the previous imposing duality of fear as a lie, an obsidian reflection made for the shadow world to sustain itself on the backs of its oft obscured objects. It was only after having gone so far in avoidance that I could now travel back directly to where the heart of the matter sat at the center of a world of reflection, where death and annihilation crossed each other, manifold illusions made the neutral place which I embodied appear to be a finitude of endless distance, a slate which on one side was the past and the other the future that held the present in a hole, a deep canyon that paralyzed the possibility of acting from becoming real.

I had been over to the window, and wouldn't tell you anything different from being over there. I had been washed away by the pungent contents of tall bottles, blue men, little girls, and night women.

I had been in the gutter and been in the stars.

So, if this was all to end, I thought, so be it. In sincerity, (and with further misunderstanding at that point still unknown to me) I began to delight in thinking of their memory resting with me. That I was, essentially, the kicked up dirt on that dusty road, the mucus, the sweat of Malius, the slimy blood, the fat and tissue strung between the two bodies, the rock and the skull, the chain and the fence, the slumped over, dead beast, and the risen beauty . . . . I was Dallin's worry, his resignation and his certainty, his unknowing. "I am the wall that I broke through. I am my attempts to hide. I am capability and am the mind. The haunting, fucked-up edifice, the house on Old Coastal Road, windows punched out and boarded up. Paintings in the wall. Chemicals and blue flowers, half a crying face, half a waning moon. The car and the road, chimerical leaves, the buildings of the vanished University. I am the last of knowledge and the first word, the impassable gulf, the man never found, the feast, the maid's pocket piece, the buses and the child, *oh my God*, the little girl, wraith, vague angel, her immaculate little steps, oh I had so much intent, cared so much, but the war, madness, there were planes, machines refused upon the road, bleeding hands and knees, carcasses all over, thoughts about a myriad of deaths. . . . The safe house, and running through a far off field, dead-wifed and faithless. I am the other half of the plan. Welcome me, whether or not you believe. *Please, welcome me in. . . .*"

The salt wind was swirling up from the shore. Sadness brought me from my white box, my gone garden, and delivered me back to the porch front at Old Coast Road 6. Unnamable violence put my hand back in that mimetic motion of turning the handle on the front door. All that I expected to see there—shadows, residual fear, the haunting and negative pursuits—was gone. The wood creaked like old wood, drafts swept like old drafts sweep an old house, nothing more.

In the basement, nothing moved or pursued, all that terror had at least recessed, and was not hiding. It had recessed itself in me. I had no right to ever project it, no right to enter that house, peruse the rooms, and take those paintings. I could not re-live my own ghost pacing through those rooms, nor bear the consequence of what I had done tearing into the history of unknown, sacred events, so ruthless in service to myself. I thought Àisling's death had answered enough the question, but something else loomed, beginning its own pursuit from within. Sure, there was nothing more to be done, as I'd fled the house before in order to escape it.

My violations were unreturnable, they could not be undone, but I returned the poem of Àisling's passage anyway, placing it tassel up in with the rest of the pages in the cardboard box, back to its rightful place. I returned the paintings too, back on the rack inside the wall underneath the stairs. My steps, my whimpering breaths, my dried vomit, each anticipated childish act, each frantic leap in every direction, all played out for me to gather back in. The play of my actions faced me with the origin of my impossible wish of taking all you've done out of time and space and pouring it, reversely, back in through your eyes, back in with all the un-became, the never-did, and the never-again.

Undergoing that, I succeeded by failing, whispering a faint, cheap prayer to return sacredness to the house, that it may again regain the purity of an unobserved truth. Naïvely, I thought my presence had been negated from ever effecting the house again, by walking out the front door, sealing the lock with heavy closing eyes, and turning away.

In gale out on the road I stood swaying with the grasses, coughing weakly (as was now custom), staring far down the beaten road to its end, where a small dune of sand began, where old, faded pavement stopped, and colored dinghies and bench-seated skiffs sat faced down on their bows. Further past the boats and the sand of the resident's cove, there stood the lighthouse. Dallin's voice no longer accounted this image for me, like a foghorn warning of my imperceptions. I needed no poetry imported to me then. Doubled in pain, the wind and whipping beads of rain, I needed no incantation, for the image stood there blatant and exact. Its gray column turned into the sky, hoisting a circular, metal cage at its top, where a beacon light blinked continuously.

All that had occurred and I had never even noticed it down there, never even saw what magnificent truth sat at the end of Old Coastal Road. It was like looking down the plane I spoke of earlier, but in the other direction, away from my house of calcified fear. It was only possible to view the lighthouse in this certain way at this point by it being in the exact opposite sphere of that house of ruin. I was caught there in a perfect exchange, balanced between the beaconing tower and the fading terrain of memory.

Images folded together, shone off the backs and sides of each other, precisely, like a diamond. One object, no center, breaking apart light, sending it off everything else and ultimately itself. Everything out there produced an incalculable number which at its origin was reducible to one. One visage, one breath, one cell, one mind, one bulb, one thought, one action of one life shot out, refracting itself into endless experience: one object, no center, forever.

Standing there, it appeared so clearly what the bathtub, the residue, the containers, and the melted curtain all meant.

After Aìsling's death Dallin returned to their house, the one that stood beside me, and submerged his body in the bath, where the chemicals dissolved his body into silt. Forfeiting the flight, imprisonment, the slow decay of life without his wife, and the probing of his own dead body; the finding of an undiscoverable man. This was how he kept his promise, rising to meet her.

"Yes, I am their death, I keep it. Aìsling is alive inside all things, I can see it now. Love's creed in long & bright stars, in wind, sea, and trees. She is here. Glory's face upon me." I spoke, and saw from the bottom of that endless movement. Yet, my breathing still diminished under an enormous, impending weight; or, an absence of weight, a lightening. Both pressure and divide, the burden and its lessening. "I am so near, having been sanctioned and allowed to pass. Having been made being and place, I am all being, and am all space, dark, light, death, all life." From within surfaces this unknown calling, from beyond, my name blinks and wavers, "Dallin." Then, it is repeated, and vibrates its way in, "Dallin, *Dallin* . . ." forcing my eyes to open.

EPILOGUE

In my last bed I lay, wrapped in linen.

Sure, I transmuted through the bay window out over the Atlantic and to the horizon. Sure, I rode light, even in darkness I was still able to transgress my tomb and miss my wife Aìsling in whichever breeze I please. But, as you know, sickness consumed me, gradually, kept me here for a stretch in my rickety drinking body, my last mortal poetries. I've come to resemble this house on Old Coastal Road, for I too am weathered, gutted, condemned to disrepair, and have come to relinquish all ambition to dying. The details of lengthy memory have been recalled and cast away for good. Everything of my murdered wife has been re-lived and now I've only one way left to regard her, *here*, where shore winds rip and turn through winds themselves, through houses, trees, and withered men. Where that old lighthouse blinks out, steadily, . . . on & on, once, & once, which is to say, continuously. Where death's presence has now been intoned, invited to arrive in the present so that, finally, we may entwine.

Where I go then from bed to floor, where from knees I crawl up to two crystal, ancient feet, and think of the feast the chemicals will have with me. . . . In the bathroom. Solitary chamber procession. Dumping empty deadly jugs that say bleach, ammonia, and lye. The tub fills fine. I disrobe. "Life took its incomprehensible time," I say, "and as with you, Aìsling, my dying is now mine."

Fragile bones move with tidal sound arcs. Feet plant then bend along a plush red carpet flush with translucent pain. A tired self machine grinds last movements through space, inching, cross carpet cross floor, through the hallway for the last time. Thoughts are bulbs & few, how Aìsling smiles in the dew-fields of new, the fields *beyond* that the death-faced are allowed to get to, where all time smiles greenly in a ring shaped bow, silent, where all godly dead watch, which perpetuates all watching. Not mistaken with last rites, a shoulder in a mirror shows itself when its covering comes loose, my pale bone grid shivers and flexes, in, then out; a sickly bird ready to go.

Two hand bouquets dip the lithe tips of their crumbly flowers in below the churning bath, the shoulder spoken of follows shortly after. Bone knees and gentle genital trees whimper. Skin peels from old toes like a woman shedding a fleece. Eyelets open along the femur, tempering out old weaknesses and sutures. Stomach hears the alkaline tide swell in off the bobbing wreckage of bridgework and rib bones and devours itself from the inside alone. Blue infant at my center-knot bleeds, then breaks apart. Reduced further. Lungs conflate, the last of the air effuses its way out the shipwrecked esophagus and mouth. The reflex of my scream lets out all over, my ears submerge in water, acids, the fluent liquid, . . . it is then that I go under.

All earth quit. Yeah, shit quit. My scream tapers as hearing joins the faculties of the past. Breath ends immediately after, as tub and corrosive compound become my grave and passage.

No longer am I in bath, house, or island beach.

The substance immersing me is *breathing*, rising, falling, and repeating, teeming with the yes and yes-no of a magnificent totality. This substance-being emerges, whose face, after I realize its absence, stretches the entire darkness about me. Its body, endless drapery. I see it near and far there, without eyes. I smell its presence, floral and base, without nose. I sense its exonic mastery, its macro-spatial temporality, and the same its hiatus from time. I become the stasis of our meeting me completely and for the first time sense all that was & is, isn't & was not, *without body*. I become its encompassment, the full immersion of all proximity. He who dwells has returned to the valley at the center, the beginning, and the end of time. Intuitively, I seek particulars; velvet chair, armoire, mirror, sink, faucet, familiar mental pantomimes. Reach underneath to feel an absent bath or even brush an absent bed, but all is around and all is none. Aligned in the god-chimes, sound vibrates and mutes itself alike. I become part of the breathing and teeming by coming face to face, which of course, is a turn-of-phrase, but in submergence with it I come to recognize myself from without, and let my body cast out the last lingering sentiments of doubt that the heavens would just not tolerate. These were the hooks and pitch-bends, the changes of substance that encircled me and circled in me until there was no distinction. What immerses me reveals its empty face, meeting the lasting lines and contour of my own. The interior of his absence meets the last of my presence exact, and we begin, minutely, to dance. We compound, lay flat, stretch, exchange in the medium of language's intention, within the silent space throughout, we fluctuate and become, at once, fluidly emergent. Only we did, we heard, only we saw, we spoke. "I am this and am this we." "Who are you?" "... I? Ha, am An Dantomine Eerly. Ha, ha ha."

Oh, An Dantomine Eerly, where does hope in the future lie? There is no future, now. I know, but for those who concern about the future? Well, poet, does the hope of the future still rests atop the leaves? Whitman would agree. Oh, would he? I could go on. . . . You know what I mean. Yes, I know what you mean. Monumental events are occurring all around us, how do you feel? I feel fine. As though you were never born, and did not just die? I've no discretion for my insides or outsides, I feel as though things are—, as though things are what? I feel as things are. That sounds essential. Sacred trees and specious night birds and men are—, Are what? Well I just don't know what it is that men believe they are doing. The technology, industry, domineering systems of value and exchange, and those crowded, stinking cities; dying in a world they toil to contrive. Yes, but that really has nothing to do with you now, does it? No, it doesn't. It's a dream as anything else, as this? Mostly that's correct. And all these dreams form in layers, called night, . . . right? Which is where we are? Which is where you have been all along. But whose sentient strains brushed by you for endless fleeting hours—, What?, spent finagling poems into rigid, thankless monuments to sorrow, exuding logic-steam into the previously weightless peace of contented drifting and dreams? It is mind that was forbidden from life for so long, it is true time—, Timelessness?, that was conspired against; terrible existence was no wonder. Exactly that, without wonder. A lapse in wonder reigned, a time of rootless paradigms reigned. Expectedly, your souls wander, you're damaged and scared, taught strange, lullful ideas about man's creation as a model in the clouds, pulled from the Deity's creational hands by earth's calling too early, man undone was left to keel apart, split between perfect, oppositional poles of nature, man began a lengthy explanation of himself based on the ruin that encompassed him, he thought this ruin was deserved, *divine* even! Man used his ruin to explain himself, and hence ruin himself through the symbol of himself as ruin, then all this language fell in line praising a minute misconstruency, a tiny, horrific distortion that man, who beholds consciousness—, More rightly partakes but Okay, the creative power of image, the god-beheld factory of imagination, powerful, microcosmic creation, could suffer for this and subsequently ban himself from the possibility of himself. The precedence for perfection in nature was obliterated—the diamond, decahedron, nautilus, golden whathaveyous, the star map, rose-essence, plasts & clons, symmetry, a love-smile fractal, astringency, spontaneity, reignless order—and was replaced with the body of God bleeding on planks of wood, the balance of bitter and blissful was separated into opposite bodies, no longer complimentary to a completeness that we beheld, but offered then as the condition for a true life that we did not and by definition could never possess, do you see the sickness? The murderers got people to thank them for murdering! Murder justified itself as contributable to progress, became even, progress itself! So then, too, we ravaged ourselves, war-torn to death. So plagued by this, far worse than nature's miseries, it was no wonder—birth into this earth now a sin—that man fell like a bleating mule accepts expiration, into life seen as a condemnation, creating then, salvation, but the continuance of that life precludes possession of that very salvation!, part rejects whole, pole denies pole, from inside to out, all balance led astray. Man's new idea was one of hysterical derision, one of inversion, an inward gazing shadow den of run-about abuses. The universe expressing its disagreement with man's conscious direction; the great, unifying order, of which we are only part, but a *whole* part. Not cog; collective network. Men gave up on the idea that they were born into perfection, inventing sciences, methods to probe, in order to refuse that a total harmony of birth and terror held them all around, they began inventing systems justifying the success & failure of each new interpretation, so to subdue his fear, the human fear of itself, of nature, of what lay beyond his realm, man lost sight that he already possessed space and the varying constructions of time, through the inheritance of universal comprehension, an inherence that defies by its very function all possession. With the birth that man's recognition instills in all that surrounds him he beheld so necessary light, and with it the *endless phenomenal unfolding* of space by light's guide, *this is time*, unfolding outward galaxy and inward kingdom alike. By light's unfolding man carried himself into the blackness of night, and then back, and each time he did this he recovered something, and as he extended his knowledge his knowledge expanded him, like a horizon broadened by vantage alone, already whole, god-like, and zenith. All has already blossomed, and we with it? Is that true? Truths are currently tightly bound up in mysteries that the lock-box of our own logic created, that our will's own unwillingness forbade us. Do you dare advance upon them? Do you dare wait patiently, even if forever? You mean, for the rest of time? For the rest of the time which is required. There is a precedence for perfection in me, you are it—, No longer are you "a worn out nightmare that is extremely exclusive," a regrettable lie of time proceeding by with or without you, the cradled infant grown old & charging off alone towards Judgment, your thoughts and all your congenial actions are no longer held from fruition by fear, no longer are you a regatta of great acts restricted by profound un-realization, no longer are you perfection corroded by gains, losses, or pride, you are here, love, here in time, with me, in sky, and night, here, in the various unifying realities of mind.

Many things have their trajectory set for you, friend, and I am so happy and sorry. What could be said to make it better? Climb the tallest hill you can see yourself at the top of and yell it out to me, make ballads of night-cries and real, essential speech, then hand them up to thee, hand them up and they will not fall back upon you, they will not return forcefully with injury and no reply as to why, no, they won't, know why? Gods sit above your head and inside, waiting to catch what you break apart into, drop, or hold out to the sky, you are slowly being catalogued in heaven my worried companion, you have to understand, there is a perfect reward for the balance you occupy, but hold out no hand for shit debts or gifts please, if I see you beg my seat will wet, our ears will grow furious with heat, please, see that they do not. Keep mouth closed and tongue inside when the fruits are falling and the violets are blooming and some ominous hand of fortune promises sweet flours and virgin pies and wine, keep those clumsy hands down, timid, scared, shitless one, quaking in the corner, hiding away from the seamless midnight sheets and cold inquiries of wind. Where is it that you play, anyway? I've never seen it this whole time. Where'd *your* rocks get off? How far up do *your* legs dampen? How strongly do you feel about the spite within? How do you react to the various forces that pinch and pain your flabby flesh sack? How many hands you've held have you given a memorizing gaze? How does it feel when lost luck lacerates the spirit? What are you even doing toying with luck so that it will deliver the best of life's secrets to you? They have to be earned, lost, given up, then found. And somewhere in there luck will choose you when you appear in its math, and its math is vast, universal, meticulous, and of course, correct. Have you ever tried to approach a periphery? It is where my nocturnal vision now bends permanently and I've never seen you there either, at times of quiet, out in the ether, neither their nor at the center. You'll have to go to the end of yourself to find out where you begin. You'll have to approach the edge to be allowed in the center again. It is there I blow huge flares of will and the sediment of good remorseless sentiment into the air to attract the wandering gaze of hand-memorizers, serene wayfarers interested in straying and staying in place, who would see at once deathly terrains within life-fields, who would know the value of the sky once they got up into it, who'd know then that there is sky within themselves where birds go and whole legions of other people look to stare and cry and pray, who realize the gift of having eyes, having ears to hear their cries, and answer back some of those prayers, pick hot stones of brilliance and burden from the deathful interstices of cold out there. Where have your aspirations gone, dreamer? Dried up child? Where have your knees crawled *you* lately? What gentle things have lately received your love, without scorn or reprieve? Do you even know how to tell what desperate things *are* desperate, and what loveless things desire most? Don't tell me about labor, don't tell me about occupations, childhood, or predispositions. Be honest, knave. Let the useless center of every argument devour the space of your face, *please already*, only is it then that I will see you, when you stop talking it is then that I can hear you, it is then that you will be truly noticeable, known to everything . . ., and there we can talk in the hazily clear space beyond speech that older great titans already told us of, where our eldest wisdom and genderless passion and elated child rest, then play, then rest again too . . ., in the place beyond weep that is deeper yes than the lowest deep but mild and lukewarm and pleasant it is; nothing merely *seems to be* on the round mounds of eternity. *Peace is not a dream*, my short-attentioned waker. I only call you new things because I cannot know you, because you still refuse that you are made up of something other than everything. I call you a friend, then ignorant of love, a merchant of rest, a faithless child, an expressionless player, a wrinkle in a hapless dream, because you are nothing and are known to none but one, and I will dress you in suits of serenity until you believe in behaving *flawlessly*. . . . Would you move with me, "just like this?" Move a little, "yeah, just like that?" A bit over there, I go here, you go there? Would you dare, nameless one? How about it? To join eternity, and never return to that cruddy world again? If we could just get down to the point here I really think you'll love it, just don't forget him when you're done reading, *ha!* sky is plums without trees breath without withered wheeze all color structure structurelessness sensation temperature pain and relief I am comfortable enough to tell you now, just watch me begin here one moment, please . . ., just watch me begin, watch it all in wonder, then watch it all again . . . I am now comfortable enough to tell you that you can find me at the end you can find me exactly where . . . this is what friends tell friends I could comprehend the rest of everything else when all time is expendable but I posit nothing new I wait for you to find me by then I'll have more to tell you watch me begin and you'll know where it ends keep reading long after I've gone promise not to be long keep

reading long after I've gone into what's happening around you you will need to know you will need to see you will need to believe in everything in order to be free things bring you happiness that you could not conceive believe me yes keep going out there stretching out and we will collide in peace just know I've gone and not returned where home is where cycles end begin and end and then begin there in the middle and on the ends down there up there where the truth is.........................
....
....
....
....
....
....
....
....
....
....
....
....
....
....
....
....
....
....
....